I GOT SENT HOME FROM SCHOOL TODAY. WITH A NOTE. FROM the vice-principal (You always know it's princi-*pal* instead of princi-*ple* because the princi*pal* is your *pal*. Right? Right.) It says I have to bring a parent along for a meeting with him tomorrow morning.

Until then I'm not allowed to go inside that school. Not even if I *wanted* to. They would stop me. What it means is, I'm suspended.

I was never suspended from school a day in my life. I was never even late, unless I had a note. Suspended. Me. I can't get over it.

I'm a criminal.

JERRY SPINELLI is an editor and writer. He lives in Pennsylvania with his wife and six children.

ALSO AVAILABLE IN LAUREL-LEAF BOOKS:

SQUARE PEGS, *Marjorie Sharmat*

I SAW HIM FIRST, *Marjorie Sharmat*

HOW TO MEET A GORGEOUS GUY, *Marjorie Sharmat*

HOW TO MEET A GORGEOUS GIRL, *Marjorie Sharmat*

RONNIE AND ROSEY, *Judie Angell*

SECRET SELVES, *Judie Angell*

THE OUTSIDERS, *S. E. Hinton*

THAT WAS THEN, THIS IS NOW, *S. E. Hinton*

TEX, *S. E. Hinton*

RUMBLE FISH, *S. E. Hinton*

SPACE STATION SEVENTH GRADE

Jerry Spinelli

LAUREL-LEAF BOOKS

Published by
Dell Publishing Co., Inc.
1 Dag Hammarskjold Plaza
New York, New York 10017

Laurel-Leaf Library ® TM 766734, Dell Publishing Co., Inc.

ISBN: 0-440-96165-3

RL: 5.3

Book Club Edition

Reprinted by arrangement with Little, Brown and Company
Printed in the United States of America
September 1984
10 9 8 7 6 5 4

for my mother and father
and brother Bill

CONTENTS

Food   3
The End   19
School   21
Hair   24
Girls   32
Football   34
Birthdays   46
Hayrides   53
Halloween   66
Trouble   73
Punishment   78
Pimples   86
Grandmothers   92
Snow   104
Waiting   113
Presents   123
Double Dips   136
Cooking   141
Hearts   152
Spring   165
Mothers   167
Miles   175
Freedom, Baseball, Bugs, Lint   186
Little Brothers   200
Headlights   214
The Dark   217
Girl   220

SPACE STATION

SEVENTH GRADE

FOOD

ONE BY ONE MY STEPFATHER TOOK THE CHICKEN BONES OUT OF the bag and laid them on the kitchen table. He laid them down real neat. In a row. Five of them. Two leg bones, two wing bones, one thigh bone.

And bones is all they were. There wasn't a speck of meat on them.

Was this really happening? Did my stepfather really drag me out of bed at seven o'clock in the morning on my summer vacation so I could stand in the kitchen in my underpants and stare down at a row of chicken bones?

"Look familiar?" I heard him say.

"Huh?" I said. I wasn't even sure he was talking to me. I wanted to go back to sleep.

He said it again. "Look familiar?"

"What?"

He swept his hand over the bones. "These?"

"What about them?"

"Ever see them before?"

"See what?"

"The bones."

"What bones?"

"*These* bones!" he sort of yelled.

He picked up a leg bone and drummed it in front of my eyes. "I know you did it, Jason."

"Did what?"

He stuck the bone under my nose. I could smell it. "Jason. I *know* you did it."

I called out, "Mom. I'm tired."

My mother sang in from the dining room, "Don't call me-ee —" like I was some stranger.

My stepfather said, "Know how I know it was you, Jason?"

"Me what?" I said.

"You who ate the chicken. *My* chicken. For *my* lunch."

"No."

"I'll tell you then." He counted on his fingers. "One: because it wasn't Mary. She hates chicken." (Mary is my cootyhead sister.) "Two: it wasn't Timmy. He doesn't steal. Yet, anyway." (Timmy is my little brother. He does too steal. My dinosaurs.) "And three and four: it wasn't your mother, and it sure as heck wasn't yours truly."

"Who's that?" I yawned.

He yelled again. "ME!"

"*Hon*-ey!" My mother's voice came floating in all sing-songy. "*Neigh*-bors."

Was this really happening?

He toned it down again. He pulled the bone away from my nose. He stared at it. He smiled at it. He kissed it. "I would have loved you," he whispered.

I wasn't surprised that my stepfather talked to a bone. Not

only is he a teacher at the community college, but he also does amateur acting. So you never know when he's serious. His name is just right: Ham. It's short for Hamilton, and it describes the way he acts pretty good too.

He went on whispering to the bone: "I would have taken you to lunch today. It would have been beautiful. Delicious. But Jason — ah — Jason did not want us to be together. He did not want me taking you away from home. He wants me to get a fast pickup at the cafeteria, not to mention a nice case of heartburn."

"Can I go back to bed?" I said.

He didn't seem to hear me. He said, "Am I that mean to you?" Silence. "Jason?"

"What?" I said.

"Answer my question, please?"

"I thought you were talking to the bone."

"Answer, please."

"What was the question?"

"Am I that mean to you?"

"What do you mean?"

"Am I a cruel stepfather?" I waited, on purpose. "Well?"

"Nah," I said. "Not really."

"Okay, so" — he put the bone down, put his hands on my shoulders — "what do you think's going to happen if you tell the truth?"

I shrugged. "I don't know."

"Think about it. Seriously." He was being the teacher now. "I'd like to know what's inside your head. Do you think I would string you up against the rafters in the cellar?" I tried to twist away but my shoulders wouldn't move. "Come on, seriously. Is that what you think?"

"Nah, I guess not."

"You *guess* not?"

"Nah. Just kiddin'."

"Well then, do you think I'm going to beat you?"

"I guess not. Nah."

"Okay. So far so good. Do you think I would — uh — throw boiling water in your face?"

"Nah."

"Put your head in the washing machine and turn it on?"

"Nah." I laughed.

"Run you over with the car? Chop your arms off? Force your mouth open and dump a thousand Brussels sprouts down your throat? Make you kiss Mary? Is that what you think?"

"I thought we were supposed to be serious," I said.

"Right. Okay — okay — now. Serious again. Just what is it you are afraid might happen if you tell me the truth? Exactly what?"

I shrugged. "Nothin'. I guess."

"Aha!" He clapped his hands. "That's right! You are absolutely right. Nothing at all is going to happen to you. Not a thing." He put the bones back into the bag. "Okay, look: we won't even talk about these anymore. Just don't do it again, okay?"

I shrugged and started to walk away. "Okay," I yawned, "but I didn't do it."

All of a sudden the top of me stopped. Then the rest of me. He was palming my head. I was stuck there facing my mother in the dining room. She was misting a fern.

Finally the hand went away. I heard the refrigerator door open. I felt the cold. I wished I had more than underpants on. I heard a strange sound. Sort of like an animal or something. Croaky. It was his voice. It turned into words.

". . . I hid it. See? There. I hid it right there . . . good as I could. I figured, I said to myself, 'Put the chicken in the bag and hide it there . . . in the crisper . . . under the cucumbers . . . and nobody will find it. Nobody. *Nobody* looks under the cucumbers. Nah. Who would look there? And then, then when you come down in the morning, there it'll be: your lunch.' But I came down" — his voice was whispery amazed — "and they were gone. I took out the cucumbers —"

I heard something plop onto the kitchen floor, I didn't have to look; I just knew it was a cucumber. Then the others came plopping, one by one. My mother was poking her head into the fern, misting like mad. I could tell she was cracking up.

"— sure enough: *gone*. And then I saw the bones." The refrigerator door closed. "Somebody . . . had eaten my chicken. But nobody did it. Sounds crazy, doesn't it?" He laughed. I pulled in my toes. "A contradiction in terms. A logical impossibility. How can something be eaten and there not be an eater? To be consumed without a consumer. Impossible, you say. Aha — but no! It has happened here. Right here in this kitchen. Sometime during the night a miracle took place. The chicken was consumed but there was no consumer." The back door twanged open. He called out. "A miracle!"

He actually did it, yelled to the whole neighborhood. Mom started pulling little brown leaves from the fern. They fluttered to the floor. The back door closed.

His voice was softer now. He just kept saying the same

stuff over and over. "A miracle . . . a miracle . . . right here in this house . . . this kitchen . . . a big fat mother of a miracle . . . right here . . ."

My mother flicked her head for me to go. Her eyes were teary from laughing. The last thing I heard on my way up-stairs was Ham saying, ". . . it's just sad, honey. Cruel really . . ." And my mother saying, "No, not cruel . . ."

So after I finally got a little sleep I heard Richie calling in the driveway.

I looked out the window. "What do you want?"

"Let's go baggin'."

We went to the A&P. We go there when we need money. Pretty soon we're going to start saving it all up, so by the time we're old enough to drive we can buy a custom van and go to California — if there's still gas.

Bagging was slow. Not many people were buying food that day. And the ones that were, were mostly men and mothers. You never get anything off them. They see you coming and they right away snatch up a bag and start doing their own. By lunch we had a measly 90¢ between us.

"What we need here," said Richie "is a flock of old ladies."

So we were splitting a soda and some chocolate cupcakes (as usual there was nothing left over for the van) when all of a sudden Richie yells "old lady!" and the soda goes spilling and the both of us go racing up to the counter where this old lady is just starting to get rung up. It's a good thing the cashier didn't turn around, because we were laughing and choking and spitting out cupcake like a couple of chocolate geysers.

The old lady didn't seem to mind. She just kept smiling away at us. I never saw her before, but I had a feeling right from the start that she was rich. You could just tell. She had this big pin like an egg on her dress. It looked like a diamond. And she had this animal slung around her neck. Dead, of course, but it still had its face and feet. The rest was brown and furry.

"Look, Rich!" I whispered. "A mink stole!"

He squinted at it. "Looks more like a fox to me."

"No, no, I'm telling you, it's a mink. I'm telling you — she's rich!"

I was even surer she was rich when I saw the lamb chops. I had a lamb chop once, and it was about the best thing I ever ate. Ham and my mother ruined theirs by putting mint jelly on them. Sometimes parents' tastes are so weird. I put good old grape jelly on mine, and that was fine. I asked Ham why we didn't have lamb chops more, and he said what he always says about everything: "Inflation." Well, the old lady had *four* of them. The rest of the stuff was mostly dog food, bottled water, and prune juice. Ugh!

After paying the bill the old lady just kept grinning and nodding away. I started thinking I might be wrong and that she might be from the state nuthouse, which is only a mile away. Then the cashier leaned over. "Why don't you guys carry her things home." He leaned over more. "She can't hear."

So Richie and me each took a bag and we almost went dancing down the street after her. Richie started saying "hey" louder and louder, but she never turned around. Then he screamed right into the back of her head: "BOO!" She didn't flinch.

"Yahoo!" I yelled. "Diamonds — lamb chops — mink! We got ourselves a millionaire!"

"What do you think we'll get?" Richie yelled.

"Millions!" I yelled. "Jillions!"

The mink face kept staring at us from the old lady's shoulder. With its black eyes all round and wide, it looked as impressed as we were. Then we saw her house. It was a row house, scrunched in between all these other skinny brick houses on this dumpy little side street.

Richie kicked me. "She ain't no millionaire." He started to put his bag right down there on the sidewalk and walk away.

"Hey, c'mon, don't do that," I said. "You can't tell nothin' by somebody's house. She's eccentric."

"What's that?"

"That's how a lot of rich people get. The more money they make the poorer they look. They don't want people to know they got a lot of money."

"Why not?"

"So they don't get robbed, hemorrhoid head."

"Okay." He poked me in the forehead. He knows I hate that. "If she don't want people to know she's rich, how come she's wearing a diamond?"

I poked him back, a poke a word. "Be. Cause. It. Ain't. Real."

That surprised him. "Huh?" he goes.

I told him, "They don't wear their real jewels outside. They wear fakes that just *look* like the real ones."

"So where's the real one?"

"In the house someplace. In a safe."

"Okay," he said, "so what about the mink?"

Just then I noticed the old lady was gone, and the door to the house was wide open. We went up the steps. "Bet it's crummy," I said. "Rich eccentrics always live in crummy houses."

Sure enough, it was crummy. Not crummy-dirty. Crummy-old. And dark. You could hardly see. I almost bumped into the mink hanging on a coatrack. The furniture was all these old antiques, and there were egg-shaped pictures of old-fashioned ladies with black dresses up to their necks, and the walls had wallpaper.

"Toldjuh," I said.

We put the bags on the kitchen table. Then we saw the cat — this humongous shaggy thing that was the craziest color — orange! — and was so fat it waddled like a duck. It just waddled over to the foot of the table and plumped down and looked up at the bags. Then before I knew what happened, the old lady whips out the lamb chops, drops one of them onto the floor — no plate — and the cat goes at it like it's ten rats.

"Man!" said Richie.

I just stared. I wanted that lamb chop.

"Man!" Richie kept saying.

When the old lady got her bags unloaded she took two glasses from the cupboard and put ice in them. *Ah, soda*, I'm thinking, but she just filled them with water and handed them to us. That smile on her face was getting a little stupid by now.

"Let's go to the bathroom," I said.

Richie's mouth got little and round and laid an ice cube. It plopped into his glass. "I don't have to go," he said.

I nudged him. "Get a look upstairs."

I turned to the stupid smile and I knew we had a problem. How do you tell a deaf and dumb old lady you have to go to the bathroom? Well, I'm standing there for about an hour moving my lips and trying to make all kinds of signs without getting too gross, and then I look over and there's Richie going *plop! plop! plop!* with his ice cubes into the water. I cracked up and we just took off upstairs. I almost broke the banister laughing.

Upstairs was scary. Old deaf lady or not, we tiptoed around. Sun was coming in here and there, but even the sun seemed dark, it was all so quiet. It was like nobody lived there for centuries.

The only thing that moved in the whole place was a drop of water coming out of a bubble on the end of a faucet (there were two of them, one Hot and one Cold). Almost every ten seconds a drop dropped, and where it hit there was this orange and green stain in the sink. It made me think about erosion. No matter how hard something is, if a little bit of water or wind hits it for long enough, like a couple million years, it will wear away. If I waited there long enough that water would drip right through the sink. That's time for you. The bathtub had squatting legs on it and there wasn't any shower.

"Where's the safe?" Richie whispered.

"How do I know?" I said. "You think she's gonna leave it in the middle of the floor?"

We looked in a couple rooms. Nothing but beds and closets and wallpaper. The wallpaper was these French poodles and fancy ladies with black pointed feet, and swans. It was all brownish-yellow. Where the edges of the paper met, little pieces about the size of cornflakes were coming off.

There was one room left, at the end of the hallway. The door was shut.

"Go ahead," I said.

Richie pushed the door open. It smelled — I don't know — old. It was dark. Three windows had long green shades pulled all the way down, even below the windowsills. But the shades had these little pinholes in them, like the sky at night, only it was sun coming through instead of stars, and where these rays of sunlight were crossing the room you could see millions of specks of dust just moving, moving; they never stopped.

What a crazy room! There was a giant bed, and lying down right on the bed was one of those big old-fashioned radios shaped like a tombstone. There was lots of other stuff too. A big stack of records. A wooden rack with these heavy black men's suits hanging on it. A row of old shoes — crazy — they went from real tiny baby shoes to big men's ones, right up the line. And next to the shoes a row of dolls, all sitting up against the wall. An old sword. An army helmet. A rocking horse. On the wall over the bed was a real long picture. It showed a bunch of dogs, big ones, and they were all looking down at this little white kitten playing with a pink ball of yarn. The funny thing was, the dogs sort of had expressions on their faces, like people.

We were looking at all this from the doorway. I pointed to the long picture. "The safe's probably behind there." I could see what Richie was thinking. "Oh no," I said, "I ain't lookin'."

Richie leaned in for a look at the side of the room behind the door. "Look," he said. "Doughnuts!"

There they were. A stack of powdered doughnuts on a silver tray. Next to lamb chops I love doughnuts. I could actually feel a hole in my stomach open up to the size of about three of them.

"C'mon," I said, but Richie was a mule in the doorway. So I grabbed hold of his shirt sleeve with one hand and stretched myself out till I could reach the silver tray with the other. I grabbed a doughnut and pulled it in.

Something was wrong. It wasn't powdered sugar.

"Dust!" Richie said.

He was right. My fingers were sunk into it. I dropped the doughnut, clapped my hands, slammed the door, and beat it downstairs all at once.

"Shit," I said in the hallway. I was even madder because I had promised myself I was going to slide down the banister on the way down and that damn doughnut corpse made me forget.

Richie said, "Look."

The old lady was sitting in a rocking chair in a corner of the living room. Her eyes were closed. She wasn't moving.

"She's dead," I said.

Then she snored.

Richie looked at me and I looked at Richie, and it was like our eyes said to each other: *We ain't getting paid.*

Richie said, "Wanna steal the diamond?" He was all excited. Then he remembered. "Oh yeah, it's just a fake."

So we just sort of left in a daze. When we passed the stupid wide-eyed animal on the coatrack, I gave it a smack in the face. We were a couple blocks away before I could finally admit it to Richie. "You were right," I told him, "it's a fox."

Next day me and Cootyhead went to my father's for our monthly weekend. One thing for sure: when we go there I don't have to worry about stepfathers or deaf old ladies trying to starve me. My father loves to eat, and he lets us make pigs of ourselves.

It starts right at the train station, where he meets us. We spot him right away by his white shoes; he started wearing them when he moved away. We go over. Cootyhead runs.

I walk. (Timmy's not there. He's Ham's.) Then all this hugging with Mary and handshaking — well, now it's hand-slapping — with me. Then he puts Cootyhead down and spreads out his arms and says so loud you get embarrassed: "It's all yours, kids! What'll it be?"

He means we can have anything we want to eat in the whole station. And we aren't limited to one thing either. We go a little crazy. We head off in different directions to the places we want to start at. Like me to the pizza and Cootyhead to the water ice. We get there and start yelling across the station for my father to come pay for what we got.

I walk out of there feeling like there's a hump in my stomach. Ice cream, hot dogs, candy, sodas, soft pretzels — anything I want. And every time — it never fails — by the time we get to my father's place one of us has to vomit.

My sister was the vomiter this time. After an hour or so I was ready for food again. In my father's refrigerator there's always a couple good things and a couple weird things. I love looking into it. It's not like at home. ("What are you looking for? You just looked in there two minutes ago. Did you think something appeared in there in the last two minutes? Shut the door.")

"What's that?" I asked. I always ask now. One time I chomped into something I thought was a cherry turnover and it turned out to be full of mashed chicken livers.

My father took it out and held it in front of me. He pulled it away when I went to touch it. "Ten dollars and ninety-five cents a pound," he goes. My father does that a lot, tells you the price of a thing instead of the thing. He was looking at it like grandparents look at babies.

I didn't even know if it was meat or fruit or what. It was sort of shiny and wet and in thin slices and orange-pink. Somewhere in color between a basketball and Cootyhead's face when she gets mad.

I said, "What is it?"

"Lox," he said.

"What's that?" I said. Crazy name.

"Fish."

"Fish? I never heard of it."

"It's smoked."

That sounded strange. "Smoked? What do you mean?"

"They build a fire under it and let the smoke flavor it."

"Who would want to do that?" I asked him.

This thin little grin came over his face. His eyelids lowered. He put his hand over the fish like he was healing it. "Jews," he said.

Ah, well, that explained it. Sort of, anyway. See, my father, since he moved out, wants to become a Jew. "Bet he has a Jewish girlfriend," was the first thing my sister said. I don't think so. I think it started with the delicatessens. Delicatessens are sort of Jewish grocery store–restaurants. They're famous for sandwiches. Well, when my father went to live in the city, he found it was crawling with delicatessens. And there's one way my father is just like a kid: he can eat all day. "Found a new deli," he's always saying happily.

So I guess my father figured if the Jews could come up with delicatessens, they must have a lot of other good stuff going for them too. So he decided he wants to be one.

But I guess it's not so easy. As far as the Jews are concerned, my father says, everybody who's not a Jew is a

Gentile. Everybody. Whether you want to be or not. Me and an African pygmy and an Eskimo — we're all the same to a Jew: we're Gentiles. If there are any Martians out there, they might not know it, but as far as the Jews are concerned, they're Gentiles too.

So you see, it's almost impossible to *become* a Jew. If you weren't born one, you can practically forget it. You can't sneak in either, because the Jews can spot a Gentile a mile off. Funny thing, though, if you're a Gentile and a Jew happens to be standing right next to you, you probably wouldn't even know it. To look at them, they seem just like us. But I don't know . . . when you hear about some of the weird stuff they do. . . . Like, they eat fishballs. In a soup! And they wear these little beanies in church — which they go to on *Saturday*. I also heard they're scared to death of pigs; they think pig meat's poison to them. (Well, personally, I don't know about that. Maybe it's true about the adults, but there's a Jewish kid in my math class, Marty Renberg, and he eats in the dining hall with the rest of us, and once I saw him eating a BLT and he didn't keel over.)

Anyway, the main thing about Jews is "life," according to my father. He says they used to throw fire and apples into the air. And they dance in a circle and smash glasses with their feet when they get married. There's something he says almost every time he's sitting in front of a mile-high corn beef sandwich with Russian dressing. He says it real slow and serious: "The — Jew — knows — how — to — live." And then he sinks his teeth into the sandwich, and the Russian dressing oozes out and runs a little down his chin.

When I think about what would happen if my father ever manages to become a Jew, I wonder mainly about two things:

1. Would that make me Jewish too?
2. What about Christmas?

At first I used to think the Jews had it really bad because they don't have Christmas. But then I heard they came up with their own holiday about the same time. It's called Hanukkah. There's no tree or trains, but they do get the best part: presents. One present a day for eight days. Now, that may not sound so hot, but I talked to Marty Renberg and he says maybe you only get eight, and maybe they come at you slow, but every one of them is a winner.

Later that night we all walked to a deli. My father had to get a bagel to make a sandwich with his lox. Mary asked him if he was a Jew yet.

"'Fraid not, Peanut," he said. "They won't let me in." He was sad.

We went into the delicatessen and got the bagel, but as usual my father wanted to hang around the meat and salad counter awhile. He was pointing out the different stuff to us, pronouncing their names in Jewish. You could tell that made him feel a little better. I started thinking about my father's teeth chomping into those corn beef sandwiches, and how bad he wanted to dance and smash glasses. Then I remembered that the Jews go to church on Saturday, and *this* was a Saturday, and we were in a *delicatessen*, and my father was almost even *kneeling* down in front of the counter like it was an *altar*, and he was saying *Jewish* words and I thought to myself all happy: *Hey, Dad — you made it! You are one! You're in!*

THE END

I CAN'T BELIEVE IT. SUMMER'S ALMOST OVER.

Summer has a funnel shape. It seems real wide at first, and deep. Slow. Like it will last forever. You just float on top of it.

But all the time it's getting smaller and smaller. And before you know it the summer days are getting sucked down faster and faster. You're helpless. You can't stop it. You're like a bug in a toilet that was just flushed.

One sure sign that summer is coming to an end is that I start liking the kids on the corner again. There's these little kids that always play on the corner in the warm weather, and I'm sort of their hero. Like, they always stop me when I'm going by on my bike and give me paper and ask me to make them paper airplanes, which I'm an expert at. I also have to settle their little arguments and all.

Early in the summer I don't mind it much. Then it gets to be a drag. But then, I kind of start liking them all over again. I guess because I know that as long as they're out there playing on the corner, summer isn't over yet.

Baseball: you can feel it dying. Every morning we meet at the field in the park: me, Richie, Calvin Lemaine, Peter Kim, and Dugan. All day we play. We can feel September closing in. We hit a little harder, run a little faster, stay a little longer. We try to squeeze out of the summer every base hit left in it. So far I have two hundred and forty-seven homeruns this year. (I keep track.) I'm shooting for last year's record of two hundred and ninety-five.

I get home and I kind of don't want to wash. Because I know the day is coming when I'll have to wait nine months to get this dirty again. When I oil my glove and put it away in the shoe box — that's when baseball will be officially over.

I ride my bike more now, when I'm not playing. I go farther and farther from home.

I guess my biggest regret is that another summer is gone and I still didn't learn to spit between my teeth like Dugan.

SCHOOL

THE FIRST WEEK OF SCHOOL IS OVER. I HATED IT. I'M NOT GOING back.

I wish I was back in the sixth grade. I was important there. I'm nothing here. I'm a turd.

They had us fooled for a little while, the teachers. "Welcome to all our new seventh-graders," the principal said over the intercom.

The woodshop teacher, Mister Slatter, gave us a little speech. He told us to relax and sit on the edge of the bench if we wanted. He smelled like sawdust. His eyebrows were golden from it. "You are not boys anymore," he told us. "From now on you are on the road to adulthood. You left your childhood back in grade school. You can kiss it goodbye." He saluted out the window. "You are in junior high school now. You are . . . *young men*."

Hah! I was a young man for about half an hour in woodshop on Wednesday. Then I had to go to the bathroom. The door didn't say Young Men. It said Boys. As soon as I opened it a ninth-grader took a cigarette out of his mouth and said,

"Watta you lookin' at, faggot-face?" I walked out. For the rest of woodshop I was sawing wood and having to pee. The more I had to pee the faster I sawed. Young man, monkey dung.

The teachers don't run this place, neither does the principal. It's the ninth-graders. You can tell a ninth-grader a lot of ways, like size and deep voice and all, but the main way you can tell them is their eyes. They don't see you. It's like they're blind to the sight of seventh-graders. They're always talking loud and laughing to each other and shoving each other, and their eyes are always off in the distance; always down the hallway somewhere like they're looking for more ninth-graders, or girls or something. If you're a seventh-grader, even standing right in front of them, you're invisible. I saw a seventh-grader, a puny little kid even for seventh grade, and he was standing in the hallway when a mob of ninth-graders came running up. They just went right over him. Never turned back. Like he was grass.

I didn't get run over yet. Mostly it's just eyes, zooming up and down the hallways over your head, like you're in a shooting gallery of eyes. Pray one of those eyes don't hit you. It happened to Richie. He was going along being invisible with the rest of us when all of a sudden he got hit by a ninth-grader's eye. We were in the bathroom. I was in one of the stalls, sitting down, but I could see out because there was a little round hole where the latch used to be.

I could see Richie right across the way. He was standing at a urinal. He just got started when some ninth-graders came in. Well, right away they start saying stuff, like, "Hey, look, we got a dingle-dick in here!" And "Leteem alone. He's tryin' to find it!"

I froze. I was thinking, *Richie, you're dead.* All I could see was the back of him, all hunched over and looking down and not moving a muscle. I made a vow to use a stall even when I had to go standing up.

Then some of the ninth-graders stepped up to the urinals. That made a problem, because now all the urinals were used up but there was still one ninth-grader that had to go. I stopped breathing.

This one ninth-grader — the backs of his sneakers were slit down to the soles — went up to Richie and put his face about one millimeter from Richie's ear. Richie didn't even look up. Just hunched over. I think he was in a coma.

The ninth-grader took his face away and just sort of stood there, next to Richie. Actually he even backed off a couple steps. *Good*, I thought. Then I saw it: this sparkling yellow stream going from the ninth-grader's pants down to Richie's right sneaker.

It's funny how you act sometimes. Like when me and Richie met outside the bathroom, nobody said a thing about what just happened. We just talked about geography class. We said everything we knew about the continents, plus Australia. But you still couldn't help hearing the sneaker squooshing away every step down the hall.

In grade school, if you had asked me what a classroom was like, I would have said "boring" or "hot" or maybe even "interesting." Now, with all these ninth-graders in the hallways and bathrooms, I have a new word for a classroom: *safe*.

HAIR

I DON'T KNOW WHY, BUT I'M THINKING ABOUT HAIR ALL THE time these days. All I have to do is hear somebody say the word and I start laughing. The same thing is happening to Richie and a lot of other guys.

At first I thought it was just me. It started the first time we had to get a shower after gym class. I guess I knew the time would happen sooner or later, but I still didn't like the idea. I had a secret plan to just get dressed and put some water on my hair, but the gym teacher kept hanging around.

It was like I didn't have any control. My eyes kept looking at the teacher and my hands kept taking one thing after another off my body. I was getting nakeder and nakeder and nothing I could do about it.

When the last thing came off I quick put the towel around me. I sort of hung around my locker, finding stuff to straighten out and all.

Then the teacher hollered: "Six minutes!"

I went over to the shower room. (Why can't they have bathtubs?) Onto the tile. I took the towel off but I still had it in front of me. I folded it, with it still in front of me. I

24

looked around for a place to put it. There were no towel racks. I'm always getting yelled at for throwing towels on the bathroom floor at home. Now when I wanted a rack . . .

"Five minutes!" the teacher called.

I put the towel down. The whole universe was eyes. It's like a million people are waiting hours just for me, and I finally come out onto a balcony and everybody is staring up because I don't have any clothes on. My butt felt like the Hindenburg and there was this elephant trunk hanging down in front of me. I was afraid to look down at it. One of the frosted windows was open and I could see this shiny silver airplane against the clear blue sky. I wondered if they could see me.

"Four minutes!"

Into the shower. Steam. Splash. Tile. Skin.

I took a peek down. I was surprised at how small it was. While I was looking down I bumped into somebody. Felt like a warm fish. Ugh.

I went to one of the showers and stood under it. That's all I did. I figured I'd get into soap some other time. The main thing was, I didn't turn around. As long as my front was facing the wall I felt a little safer.

I got out almost as soon as I went in. As I was leaving I noticed a funny thing: everybody else was facing the wall too — all backs and butts. I dried off in about one micro-second. I didn't have to touch my back.

Then something funnier started happening during the next couple weeks. Kids started turning around. Two or three new ones each shower. I sure didn't want to be the first, but I didn't want to be the last either, so one day I turned around too.

Hair. That was the first thing I noticed. Joe Sorbito had

pubic hair. Lots of it. All black like his head. He looked like my father. (I never saw my stepfather yet.)

What's funny is, Joe Sorbito is little. He's one of the littlest guys in seventh grade. And he's not older than everybody else either. He just has hair. It's a weird feeling being in the same shower with him, especially if it happens to be just the two of you. It's like I thought he was like me but I found out he's not. It makes you feel like a little kid again.

I watched him drying off. It's under his arms too. I wonder what it's like. What does he know that I don't know? Since last Wednesday I see Joe Sorbito in class and in the hallways; he still wears the same clothes, but he's not the same Joe Sorbito I used to know.

Richie shocked me one day. Out of the blue he goes: "McGinnis has hair."

"What do you mean?" I said.

"He got hair. Pubic hair."

Richie's in a different gym class. We never talked about this before. "Down there?" I said.

"No, on his feet, turdbrain."

"Arms too? Pits?"

"Yep." He looked proud.

"Sorbito too," I said.

"Yeah?"

"Yeah."

"I ain't surprised," Richie says.

"You ain't? Why not? He's just a little dude."

"He's Italian."

"So what?"

"They get theirs faster. Them and black guys."

I was surprised he knew all this. I'm usually the one that knows things. I said, "Where'd you find out all this?"

"My mother."

That was weird. I'm going to have to take a closer look at Richie's mom.

"So McGinnis is Italian, huh?" I said.

"He ain't black," Richie said.

"So I guess Calvin has it then, huh?" I said. Our friend Calvin Lemaine is black.

"Guess so."

Then I brought up Peter Kim, who's Korean.

"Ever see a Korean with a beard?" Richie said. I couldn't think of any. "They don't get hair," he said.

"No?"

"Nope. Nowhere. Just on the head."

I said, "Dugan?"

I figured Dugan would be a problem. We don't know much about him except he's Catholic. Nobody was ever in his house. When you're going someplace, he just shows up.

But Richie had an answer for Dugan too. "Probably does."

"How's that?"

"Catholics. They're usually hairier than Protestants."

We started to count the guys we knew had hair in our gym classes. The final count was three in my class, four in Richie's.

"That's seven," I said one day. "How many do you think there are in the whole grade?"

"I don't know," Richie said. "Maybe twenty. Twenty-five."

"So how many blacks are there?" We counted them up. "Five. That leaves twenty Italians." I thought for a minute. "But how do you know which ones they are? Unless you see them in the shower?"

"Their last name ends with i or o," Richie said.

"Yeah?"

"Yeah."

"That's Sorbito."

"Yep."

"Well, what about McGinnis then?"

"He must be northern Italian."

"What's that?" I said.

"He's from North Italy." Richie was pointing, to North Italy I guess. "They're still Italians but they're a little bit like us."

"What are we?"

"Anglo-Saxton."

I don't know where his mother's getting all this stuff. "I never heard of that," I said.

"Well, we are. We're wasps."

"What!"

"Yeah. It stands for White Anglo-Saxton Protestant. W-A-S-P."

Live and learn. I always thought wasps were skinny bumblebees.

That night I asked my mother, "Am I a wasp?"

"No, you're a grasshopper," says Cootyhead.

"Mom?"

"You certainly are," she says. "And proud of it."

So the next day I said to Richie, "So if you know everything, what's the difference?"

"What do you mean?"

"How come the Italians and all get their hair before us?"

"Heat," he said.

"Heat?"

"Yeah. The hotter you are the faster your hair comes in."

I *knew* Richie was stupid. "Sorbito ain't no hotter than me," I said. "I'm out in the sun all the time."

He sneered. "I don't mean that, hemorrhoidal tissue. I mean near the equator. You ever hear of the equator?"

That's what I hate about him. He always makes everything into geography. He's a geography freak. I poked him in the forehead with my finger. "I'm telling ya—"

"So," he says, "the closer you live to the equator the more hairy you get. Not you. Your—you know—where you came from. Over there."

"An-something," I said.

"Ancestors! Yeah. The Italians are south, see, they're closer to the equator, so they get hair."

"McGinnis," I said.

He breathed. "Even North Italy is south to us."

I gave up on that. "So what's the equator have to do with it?"

"The heat, I said. The closer you get to the equator the hotter it gets."

"Heat makes the hair grow?"

"Yeah. Climate."

"So what about the blacks?"

"They're the hairiest of anybody," Richie said. "The sun fries their hair. That's why it's all frizzled."

"They must be from real close to the equator, I guess."

"Yeah!" Richie goes. "Right on it!"

"Damn!" I said. "Imagine how hot it is there!"

"Sun's always shining."

"Not *al*ways."

"A lot, yeah. They never get winter. The equator's the hottest place in the world."

"Man! Imagine going around the world right on the equator."

"Man!" said Richie.

We thought about that for a while.

Richie pulled out a Tootsie Pop. He said, "Some of them get hair by the time they're six."

I had the weirdest dream that night. I was in the shower alone with this black guy and he kept soaping up his hair until the whole shower room was filled with suds. Then he's dragging me across the soccer field and I don't have a stitch on and there's a bunch of ninth-graders grinning at the soccer backstop and my heels are making trenches in the ground because I just know there's a girl behind there.

"I had the weirdest dream last night," I said to Richie.

"Yeah? What about?"

"Ah, I don't know. All kindsa junk." We were in front of my locker, getting ready to go home. "You wanna grow up?" I said.

"What do you mean?"

"Do you want to grow *up*?"

"Do you?"

"I asked you."

"I don't know." He rubbed his fingers along the lockers. "I guess not." I felt better. "Do you?"

"Ah . . . I don't know," I said.

But I was thinking this crazy idea: if I could find some way to keep my pubic hairs from popping out, I could stay twelve forever.

Then I hear this voice: "Jason!" And footsteps running.

It was Betsy Heidenbach. She has the hots for George Dermody. She was panting. "Jason, do you have a comb a minute?"

"Why?" I said.

"Jason — quick — I *have* to get to my *bus!*" (George Dermody takes her bus.)

"Why?"

"*Jay*-son!"

I swore I would make her say it. "Why?"

Her eyes got all wide and innocent, like she didn't know what she was saying. "So I can comb my *hair*, stupid!" she yells. And she starts going through my locker.

I couldn't tell her I didn't have a comb, because me and Richie were too busy cracking up. Richie actually rolled on the floor.

GIRLS

GIRLS ARE KIND OF LIKE GOD. YOU BELIEVE IN THEM BUT YOU don't really have much to do with them.

Girls think they're as good as boys these days, in sports and stuff, I mean. But they're not. Even if a girl was a foot taller than me I could still beat her up, because men are stronger. I almost get dizzy thinking about it, but I could beat up my mother if I really wanted to. *Wanted* to. (Mothers are actually just girls that had babies.) Sometimes I think if I was attacked by a bunch of girls, even ten of them, I would — *Pah! Pah! Yongah!* — I would be too quick and strong. Even one hundred of them. It's just nature.

Besides, girls can hardly even do anything because they might go bleeding. That's one of the main reasons I wouldn't want to be a girl. Last year in the sixth grade we were having races in the playground to see who would be in the grade school track meet for the whole town. Some high school coach was in charge, and Susan Tenine couldn't even finish her race. She started to bleed. I didn't see it, I just saw this whole bunch of girls heading for the school door. The thing was, Susan Tenine was the fastest girl in school.

She could even beat some of the guys (fat ones). So she never went to the track meet.

It can hit you anytime. Imagine: riding your bike, or playing football. Or sleeping! Ugh. You have to start wearing the rag. It's like a diaper. Who wants to be a baby all over again?

Every once in a while I think about girls and growing up at the same time, and when that happens I can't help thinking about the uncomfortablest thing of all: getting married. I can't see myself doing it, no matter how old I am, but I guess I will if everybody else is. I'm not going to fight everything. I don't go around like some kids saying they're never going to change. I know when I'm a grownup I'm going to like some stuff that I don't like now. But there's two things that won't change — I swear to God — as long as I'm alive: I won't stop riding my bike and I won't get undressed in front of some wife.

Girls scream, throw funny, think they're great, and don't have anything between their legs. Girls don't wear dresses as much as they used to, but they still cry.

You know there's a girl in your family if you have to go to the bathroom in the middle of the night in the dark, and you pee on the toilet seat because it's down.

My sister isn't a girl. She's a cootyhead. I call her that because once in second grade she brought home this piece of paper saying to check her head because somebody in the school had cooties. She tries to say everybody in her class got the same note.

Ham always likes to snicker and go, "Someday you'll love your sister."

Then he says it to her: "Someday you'll love your brother."

It's the only thing me and my sister ever agree on: "Ugh!"

FOOTBALL

OUR FIRST FOOTBALL GAME WAS AGAINST CRESTHAVEN. WE LOST 19–0. We stink.

I couldn't believe it. I thought we were good. The coach said so. We were great in practice. Touchdowns all over the place. I thought we could probably do good against the Philadelphia Eagles or somebody. Then: 19–0.

The whole football thing's been a surprise to me, ever since Richie grabbed my sleeve and said, "C'mon. You're goin' out for football, ain'tcha?"

I didn't know what was happening. I thought they would just give you a football and say, "Here. Go play." But it's not like that. It's not like the street.

First thing I know I'm standing in line along with the other players in my underwear. There's a doctor up at the head of the line. He gets to sit down.

I thought there was an epidemic. Guys kept coughing. But then when I got closer to the doctor I noticed that the only ones that coughed were the ones getting examined. *That's really stupid*, I thought. *Why don't they hold it till he's done*

34

*with them? He'll think they're sick and kick them off the
team.*

Then it was my turn. Everything was going okay, and
then all of a sudden he grabs me by the gonads and says,
"Cough."

I coughed.

His bald head swung up. His face wasn't too happy.

"Not on me, please. Turn your head. Cough."

I turned my head and saw some frosted windows. I
wondered if there were girls behind them trying to see in.
I coughed.

"Again," he says.

Jeez, they just don't give you a break when you're a
seventh-grader. You can't even cough right.

"Aah — CCHHAAAH!" I go.

I must have coughed good. I got my suit. Number 41.

I didn't see Richie till next morning in woodshop. I was
working on my space station. I designed it myself. Mister
Slatter was impressed. When it's all done it's going to be as
big as a school desk. It will have everything. McDonald's.
Ping-Pong. You name it. A thousand people will live there.
Maybe five thousand.

So I'm sawing away on this piece of wood that's supposed
to be a perfect circle, and Richie whispers over, "Wha'd you
think of the physical?"

"For football, you mean?"

"Yeah."

"What about it?" Richie looked around, then pointed to
his gonads. I said, "Maybe he likes boys."

"C'mon. Why do you think they do that?"

"I don't know. I ain't a doctor." My saw was getting off-line. "Maybe they want to make sure you got two."

"Don't everybody?"

"Hell no," I said. "C'mon now, shut up. I can't saw right."

I should have saved my breath. When Richie starts asking questions he never stops.

"You mean you know somebody that don't have two?" he asks me.

"No, dumbo, not personally. What do you think, I go around staring at crotches?"

"So —?"

"So, I'm telling ya, there's some people that only have one."

"One ball!"

Mister Slatter's golden eyebrows went up. "Yes, men?"

"Nothin'. We're okay," I told him.

After a while Richie starts up again. "So what about the cough? What's that have to do with it?"

"I don't know," I said. "Maybe that's so you won't notice what he's doing with his hand."

Then he said, "Do you think the doctor does it to girls too?"

"Do girls have gonads, genius-head?"

"Well, he must do something." He put his piece of wood down and thought. "I wonder what he does."

I was trying to think up a good one, but Richie answered his own question: "Maybe he grabs their tits and tells them to fart."

By the time I stopped laughing my circle was a perfect egg.

When the coach asked what position we wanted to play, I went over with the linebackers.

"You sure you want to be a linebacker?" the coach said.

"Yeah," I told him.

"That the smallest suit you could get?"

"I don't know. It's what they gave me."

He sort of whistled. "Okay."

Then practice started and that's about the last thing I remember real clear. I know we did about a jillion jumping jacks and pushups and stuff. The worst kind was, you do like a pushup, only at the top of it you throw your arms out and come crashing right down on the ground on your stomach. It's like getting punched. This grunt pops out of your mouth. The first time I did it I grunted out both ends.

We ran. Around the field? No way. Up the bleachers. My helmet kept falling over my eyes. My shoulder pads were clapping. My kneepads kept banging on my ankles.

Somebody yelled, "Linebackers — over here!" and we started tackling this dummy (not a teacher, some stuffed bag) and then we had to tackle each other and then we ran some more. And then (I couldn't believe it) they gave us mimeographed papers to take home and study. Like homework! They were the plays.

Next thing I knew I was throwing up in the locker room. I had to crawl home. I couldn't eat. I couldn't see.

"What happened to you?" I heard my mother say, like through water.

"Football," I said. And went to bed.

Next morning Richie says, "I heard you barfed all over the locker room yesterday."

"Who told you that?"

"Kraspel."

"Kraspel? Who's that?"

"He's on the hundred-and-twenty-five-pound team."

We're on the hundred-pound team. "He don't know me," I said.

"He said it was some real little funny-looking kid," Richie smirks. "So I figured it was you."

After I beat him on the head with my biggest book, *World Geography*, he goes, "Okay. So wha'd you think of practice, huh?"

I straightened up a little. "It was okay. Why?"

"Wha'd you think the hardest part was?"

"I don't know. None of it seemed too hard to me."

"Those belly-whompers."

"So?"

"Running up those stands! Your legs hurt?"

My legs hurt so much that the only way I could keep my knees from buckling under me was to think real hard about them. It was like learning to walk again. I shrugged. "Nah. Yours?"

"Yeah, man. They're killing me. You musta had it easy."

Did he really say that? "Easy! I'd like to see you be a linebacker. *You're* the ones that got it easy. You dinky little halfbacks."

Richie made like a jive black. "Ahm gonna score me some tee-dees, Jack."

"Yeah, yeah," I said. "Running around tiptoeing till somebody touches you with the end of their finger and then you fall down. You call that football?"

"That's what I call it."

We stopped and stared at each other.

"It's pussy," I told him.

"What?"

"Pussy."

"So what's linebackers?"

"That's football, baby." I poked him in the chest. "Football."

"Down in the trenches, huh?"

"Yeah. That's right. Down in the trenches."

"Let me tell you something" — now he was poking me — "you look like an idiot out there. What're you doing being a linebacker anyway? Eighty-nine-pound linebacker."

"Ninety-two pounds."

"So? You still look like an idiot. You're gonna get creamed all over the place."

"If you can't take it, quit," I told him and got in the last poke.

The only thing that got me through the first two weeks of practice was waiting for a chance to tackle Richie. Linebacker-to-halfback. We'd see who the pussy was.

Then it came. The second strings were scrimmaging each other. Most of the time everything was a mishmash. Fumbles. Guys running the wrong way. After each play twenty-two guys were on top of each other and the ball gained about an inch.

But then came the play I was waiting for, just like I hoped it would happen for days. The quarterback handed off the ball to Richie, and Richie came through this nice big hole in the line, and there we were — nobody between us. Him and me. One on one.

To tell you the truth, I was a little surprised at first at how mean he looked. Mouthpiece showing, like a boxer. His eyes were looking through his facemask bars right into mine.

I got set. I spread my legs, lowered my butt, dug my cleats into the ground. *Now we'll see.* I charged forward to ram him back to sixth grade, closed my eyes for the collision, grabbed with both arms — only he wasn't there. I felt his toe knock my knuckles, and by the time I opened my eyes and turned around he was twenty yards up the field heading for the goal line.

I tore off my helmet and screamed: "Chicken! Chicken! Pusseeeeee!"

Then came the first real game and the 19-0 smear job from Cresthaven. I didn't get put in till they had their nineteen points, and then all I did was eat a lot of grass and dirt.

Who needs it? I'm thinking. What did football ever do for me? It grabbed my gonads, gave me pants with knees down at my ankles, made me vomit, put me on second string, embarrassed me, put cleat marks on my back and dirt in my mouth.

"I'm quitting," I told Richie.

"Quit?" he goes. "You can't quit. We just started."

"I don't care," I said. "I wanna play and all I'm doing is sitting on the damn bench. I joined this team to play some football. I'm no bench-warmer."

"But you can't quit now."

"Why not?"

"Cause our first home game's coming up."

He was right. Cresthaven was an away game. Willard would be home. But so what? All the more reason to quit. Who wants to have his friends come out and watch him sitting on the bench?

"I'm quitting," I said.

"You can't. We'll win. You always play better on your home field. And Willard stinks."

Well, I don't know why, but I let him talk me into staying. For one more game anyway. I sure am glad I did — and not for any reason Richie gave me either.

There we were in the first quarter against Willard, all of us bench-warmers warming the bench, Richie alongside of me, and all of a sudden I hear something behind us. I turn around . . . cheerleaders! A whole line of them. Only about ten feet away, between us and the bleachers. There's more of them (nine, I count) than people in the stands (three), but they're there cheering away like it's the Super Bowl or something.

I just keep looking. They have on white sweaters and crimson skirts. (They're our colors. "Crimson," you have to say. Not "red.") Then, when the cheer was over, the cheerleaders turn back to the game, facing us now, and the one that was right behind me comes ahead a couple steps and all of a sudden she jumps up in the air and pumps her arms and yells, "Go, Bulldogs!"

While the game went on I kept looking behind me more than at the field.

I nudged Richie. "Rich. Look."

He looked. "Yeah?"

"Cheerleaders."

"So?"

"Waddaya think?"

"I don't know. What about?"

"Ever have cheerleaders before?"

"No. You?"

"No."

He turned back to the game.

"Hey Rich."

"What?"

I cranked his head around. "Waddaya think of that one?"

"What one?"

"Right here. *This* one."

"Here?"

"Yeah."

"What about her?"

"Waddaya think?"

"She's okay." He turned back.

I can tell you, she was more than okay.

"You know her name?" I said.

"Nope."

"She in seventh grade?"

"How do I know? Watch the game, willya."

Around the middle of the second quarter she did something that really got to me. Trexler, our best runner, got loose on an end run and comes running down the sideline right past our bench, and next thing I know there's this screaming in my ear. It's *her.* She's not only behind me, but over me too. That's because I'm standing up with all the other guys yelling at Trexler, and what she did was jump up onto the bench where I had been sitting. And there she is yelling. "Go, Billy! Go, Billy! Go, Billy!" Her sweater is flapping over my face and I can see little spit specks flying from her mouth and even her eyes are screaming. And I know right then, just like that, that what I really *really* want is for some cheerleader — I was already praying for it to be her — some cheerleader someday to be yelling my name like that. *Go, Jason! Go, Jason! Go, Jason!*

I kept thinking about that all during the halftime meeting. And then it hit me: nobody's going to cheer for a linebacker. Who was going to notice me, down there in the trenches? You had to be out in the open, the open field, racing down the sidelines, the lunks on the other team eating your dust — *Go, Jason! Go, Jason! Go, Jason!*

"Coach," I said on the way back to the field, "can I be a halfback?"

"Hey," he goes, "tiger like you? Playing a twinkletoes position? Better to tackle than *be* tackled, right?" He smacked me on the butt. "Let's go, tiger!"

So much for that.

Then, late in the game, Morgan got hurt. His leg. He was lying out there on the field for a long time, twisting all around like he was in agony. Then a stretcher came and he was carried off the field. They drove a station wagon right up to our bench and loaded him in the back of it and took him away. To a hospital, I guess.

But the thing is, while all this was going on the cheerleader was practically going crazy. "Oh God!" she kept going. "Oh God! Oh God! Oh God!"

She really got bad when they brought him over on the stretcher and he was covering his face and moaning and all. She buries her face in another cheerleader's shoulder. "Oh *God!* I can't look. Is he okay? Please be okay. Oh God oh God oh God."

And then when they were putting him in the station wagon: "Please be okay, Russell."

And then when they drove away. Kind of squeaky: "Yea, Russell!" There were tears rolling down her cheeks.

Yeah, I thought. *That's it. I gotta get myself injured.*

Well, I did two things between then and the next home game. (Richie was wrong about Willard. They didn't stink. They beat us 13–2.)

First I found out all I could about the cheerleader. Her name is Debbie Breen. She lives on Willow Drive. She's a

general student. (I'm academic: *ahem,* college material.)
She has a little brother, like me. Her father is a real-estate
agent. She has pierced ears, wears makeup, likes boys but
nobody special, has a crush on Mister Harbison, the new
gym teacher, hates spaghetti, loves the Tilt-A-Whirl, hangs
around outside the front door till the last microsecond in the
morning, and passes me in the hallway going to classes twice
on Tuesday and Thursday, once on Monday and Wednesday,
and not at all on Friday. But I'm working on some new
routes for myself, so that's going to be upped.

The second thing I did was a lot of thinking and planning
about how to get injured. And a lot of daydreaming about
what it was going to be like when they carried me off the
field. Here's the stuff I thought about:

1. Has to be close to the home side of the field.
   What a bummer if I go and do it, then they
   carry me off to the visitors' side of the field!
2. Try to actually, really get myself injured.
   a. Just stand there and let the fullback run over
      me.
   b. Get myself between two blockers and let
      them sandwich me.
   c. Curse at the biggest guy on the other team.
3. If time is running out and I'm still okay, fake it.
   a. Empty out Contac capsule. Fill with catsup.
      Put in mouth. Bite down to look like bleed-
      ing. Like in *The Sting.*
4. Show a lot of pain. Make it look as bad as
   possible. Moan. Groan. Beat fist on stretcher.
5. Don't cry.

Every night when I went to bed I practiced keeping my
eyes just a tiny bit open, so I could see Debbie Breen's crying

face following me to the station wagon and sniveling, "Oh God! Oh Jason! Please be okay! Oh Jason!" and then burying her face in another cheerleader's shoulder and sobbing uncontrollably.

The day came. The game was against Ellis Township. I stuck the capsule in my jockstrap. Funny thing was, Ellis Township stunk as bad as us. The score was 0–0 after the first half, and it stayed that way till late in the fourth quarter. Then we scored a touchdown and went ahead 6–0.

I guess I should have been happy, but what it meant was I didn't get a chance to play. I played a little at the end of the other games because we didn't have a chance. But now the coach was keeping the first-stringers in to make sure we didn't blow it. So I had to sit there and listen to Debbie Breen scream for Trexler and all the other heroes all day long.

When the game ended, everybody on the bench jumped up and ran out to grab the guys on the field and celebrate. So I had to too. Then we all came running back, all bunched up like a herd of monkeys, and the next thing I know I'm tripping over the stupid bench and my face falls forward right into somebody's heel coming up and my whole body becomes like loose change.

I remember being on the ground and looking up and seeing these faces and helmets floating in and out of each other. If Debbie Breen was crying for me I don't remember hearing her. All I remember is somebody saying, "He got kicked in the head, didn't he?"

"Yeah, I think so."

"So what's he doing with all this blood between his legs?"

BIRTHDAYS

It's my birthday. October 15. I'm thirteen.

I'm a teenager.

In a couple minutes my mother will come into my room, open the shade, and say, "Rise and shine, birthday boy! How's it feel to be thirteen?"

Then I'll bump into Ham in the kitchen, and he'll say something really clever, like, "What? Your birthday? Uh-oh." (He always pretends he doesn't know when your birthday is, so you'll think you're not getting anything.) Or, "What are ya now — ten?" (He pretends there's so many of us he can't remember our ages.) Or, "Well, since it's your birthday, you're allowed to sneak down here and eat my lunch out of the refrigerator every night for a week." (Fat chance.)

Then Timmy will come over and say, "Hi, Jason. Happy birthday. Look at the card I made for you." So I'll have to look at this ratty piece of paper with some crayoning on it. He'll say, "Guess what it is," and I'll say a dinosaur or something just to give him an answer, and it will turn out to be a bird's nest.

Cootyhead Mary will just come down as usual, snatch up the milk, slop down her cereal, and leave. She won't say anything. Not to me anyway.

At school nobody will know it. It won't feel like my birthday even to me. Just another day of trying to shove my taped-up right eye in front of Debbie Breen and getting her to ask me about it.

Then it will start again when I get home from school.

There will be cards from all three sets of grandparents. The grandmothers, actually. They're the ones that remember. The cards will each have $2. My mother will say, "Did you *bother* to read the card?"

My father's card will come a couple days late. It will be a funny one, and it will have a homemade coupon for the present he's going to give me when I see him next.

And sooner or later, sooner or later my mother will say what she's been trying out on me for the last year or so: "Well Jason, this is the day I've been telling you about. Starting now you're going to start pulling away from your mother. The little boy who used to kiss me and bring me dandelions won't even say goodbye now when he leaves for school. He'll be ashamed to be seen with me. He'll forget to give me Mother's Day cards."

And Ham will say, "How's it feel to be a rotten teenager, Jason old boy?"

And then the worst part: Everybody (except Cootyhead of course) singing "Happy Birthday."

And then the best part: the presents. If it wasn't for them, I wouldn't go through the whole mess.

What none of these grownups know is, I've been thinking about thirteen for a couple weeks now. Getting a head start, sort of. I keep remembering this dumb thing Ham said when we were at the mall. Richie came along with us. It happened when me and Richie were at the big gusher water fountain, the one you throw pennies into. We were just sitting at the edge part, eating ice cream cones and rolling pennies back and forth to each other. If your penny veered off into the pool, you lost a point.

Then all of a sudden there's Ham standing over us. I got the feeling he was there for an hour, just watching us with this weird grin on his face. When we look up he shakes his head like he's sad and smiling at the same time and he says, "Hold on to it, boys. Life is never better than it is for a twelve-year-old boy. Right at this very moment, you may not know it, but you are living the best minutes of your whole life." And then he walks away.

I don't know what all that was supposed to mean, except he didn't know what he was talking about when he said twelve is the perfect age. Can I drive a car? Can I buy whatever I want? Can I bounce a basketball in the house? Eat both chicken legs? Stay up late? Drink beer? (If I wanted to?) Have a BB gun? Get the sneakers I *really* want? Trip Cootyhead? Burp anytime? I could list about a million.

A couple days later I asked Richie when he was going to be thirteen.

"Next year," he said. "May second. What about you?"

"October fifteenth."

"Next year?"

"Nah. This."

"Man, that's almost here."

"Yeah."

"You gonna get more allowance?"

"Probably not."

"Stay out later?"

"Definitely not."

"Hey Jason," he goes, "remember that stuff your step-father said at the mall? Weird, huh?"

"Yeah."

"Do you think twelve's so great?"

"Twelve? Nah. I had enough of it. I'm getting out. You comin'?"

"Man, I wish I could." He punched a tree. "Hey, think you'll ever be thirty?"

"That's dumb," I said. "Yeah. If I don't get hit by a truck."

"No, no. I mean, I *know* you'll be thirty, someday, but I mean" — he was grunting trying to squeeze out the words — "you know it and you don't know it. Know what I mean?"

I knew exactly what he meant. "You know it in your head, but you can't believe it's really gonna happen."

"Yeah, yeah!"

"Yeah, I know."

"I mean, I can't even believe I'm ever gonna be twenty."

"I got news for ya," I told him.

"What?"

"I'm never gonna die."

We were standing at Eagle Road, where the cars go by pretty good. I stepped off the curb. (I remembered Ham saying once, when we almost hit some kids on bikes without reflectors: "They think they're invincible. They actually believe they cannot be hit by a car.")

Richie nodded. "Yeah, I know —"

"No," I said. "I'm serious. Just think about it." I turned to him. I had to look up since he was still on the curb. "Most people died because they made some mistake. Like they ate too much cold cuts and got cancer. Or they didn't exercise and they got a heart attack."

"Or they didn't be careful crossing the street."

"Or they didn't lay down flat when there's lightning."

"Or they went swimming with sharks around."

"Yeah, right," I said. "See what I mean?"

"Or they left the car running in the garage."

"Right."

"Or they parachuted into a volcano."

I knuckled his forehead. "Right. Right. Now cool it."

"So what about old age?" he goes.

"What about it? Know what old age is?"

"What?"

"It's hardening of the arteries," I told him. "That's all. And not everybody gets it. That's the one thing you have to be lucky about. If hardening of the arteries misses you, and you don't make any of those dumb mistakes" — I stepped back up onto the curb — "there's no telling how long you can live." I let that sink in. Then I said, "Ever hear of Mathusah?"

"Who?"

"Mathusah. He's a guy in the Bible. Know how long he lived?"

"How?"

"Nine hundred and sixty-nine years. Bay-beee."

"Man!" he goes. "That's true?"

"Sure," I said. "It's in the Bible. Look: there was no cancer then, right? No cold cuts. No cigarettes —"

"No asbestos."

"Right."

"No fumes."

"Right right right. No alotta things. No cars to run you over. No airplanes crashing. The only mistake you could make was let yourself get caught in a war."

"Or go to sleep right where some camel was ready to take a shit."

I cracked up. "Right! Stop!"

"Yeah," he said. "But it's not the Bible now."

I said, "Ever hear of the guy down Florida?"

"What guy?"

"Some slave. Well, he's not a slave now. He used to be. A black guy. He lives in Florida."

"What about him?"

"What about him is, the dude is a hundred and thirty years old, that's all." Richie whistled. "Yeah, that's right. And they think he might even be older than *that*. Because they can't find his birth certificate."

"What's he do?"

"I don't know. Hangs around, I guess. They tricked him to get him out of Africa."

"Wha'd they do?"

"They told him there's pancake trees in America."

His eyes get wide. "Ain't there?" he goes.

I punched him. "You wanna talk or not?"

"So, he believed it?"

"Yeah. He was just a kid then."

"Maybe that's why he's living so long," Richie said. "He's so dumb."

We walked up to the light and waited for green. "Well anyway," I said, "all I'm saying is, this guy's a hundred and thirty years old, and if he can do it, *I* can do it."

Richie poked me. "Yeah, but you said you weren't gonna

die at all. You were gonna live forever. That's what you said."

"Yeah, that's right. I said it. Look: what's the difference between a hundred and thirty years and forever, anyway? Huh? You can't even believe you're ever gonna hit twenty. I'm telling ya —" The light was green. We crossed. "When I grow up I'm gonna start being careful: no mistakes, no hardening of the arteries, knock on wood" — I knocked on his head — "before you know it I'll be at a hundred and thirty. And then, who knows? Look at Mathusah. *Nine hundred and sixty-nine.* I'm telling ya, once you get past the first fifty or hundred years, you got it knocked!"

HAYRIDES

"Goin' to the hayride?" I asked Richie.

"I don't know. You?"

"I don't know."

It's all everybody was talking about. It was just for the seventh-graders, and it was going to be up at this place called Gwendolyn Orchards.

Richie grinned. "You're goin'."

"That so?"

"Yeah. You're goin'."

"Who says?"

"Me."

"How do you know if *I* don't even know? You turn into a mind-reader all of a sudden?"

"Nope."

"So?"

"So?"

"So, how do you know, fishfart?"

"Because somebody you know's goin'."

My face was getting warm. I stared at our bus, which was just pulling up. "Yeah? Who?"

53

He coos, "You know who."

I climb onto the bus and quick head down the aisle. But Richie's voice is following me like a fire on the back of my neck: "Debbie . . . Debbie . . ."

I think the parents were behind the whole thing, because the school was having it on Mischief Night, the night before Halloween. Keep us off the streets, I guess. Afraid their windows might get a little soapy. Or their house might get egged.

We talked about moving Mischief Night up one. But nobody did anything about it.

Anyway, it turned out we had three wagonsful for the hayride. Besides Richie, Peter Kim and Calvin came too. And Dugan showed up, of course. Even though he goes to Catholic school.

So, I'm kind of hanging away from the wagons at first, because I'm waiting to see which one Debbie Breen is getting into. She's got this lemon-yellow quilt jacket on and her face was so — I never saw her at night before — she was so perfect. She was the most beautiful girl in the universe.

Well, she finally hops into the front wagon. I pretend I don't notice, wait a minute, then I say, "Well, might as well get in, huh?"

So we pile in. By now all the wagons are loading up. Us guys are at the back of the wagon on one side. She's at the front on the other side. I pretend I don't know she's there, but my heart's going nuts.

Then the motors start up — each wagon has a tractor to pull it — and as soon as that happens there's this wild scream from the wagon behind us: "Debbie-e-e!"

And from the front of our wagon: "Jude-e-e!"

And next think I know Debbie Breen and another cheer-leader are crawling over my feet, jumping down from the wagon and running back to the next one. Hands reach down to help them climb on.

"Shit," I said into the straw.

It was a junko hayride. I couldn't wait till it was over. The ride was bumpy and the tractors were so slow I wanted to get out and walk. They kept going *puh-puh-puh-puh.* You felt like you were being dragged off to a war or some-thing.

First we went along these old skinny roads where cars hardly ever went. And when a car did go by, everybody got so excited you would have thought the school burned down. I just sat there. All I did was keep offering Dugan $1000 to moon one of the cars, but he wouldn't.

Then the wagons went off the road and up through the orchards. Next thing you know everybody's reaching out and picking apples and throwing them at everything: the wagon behind, the tractors, the trees, the moon. Never occurred to any of the idiots to eat them.

So the drivers start keeping the wagons farther away from the trees. So the big hay fight starts. Which I wasn't about to get into, except Richie jammed a fistful of hay in my face.

Once when I reached down for a handful, who's under-neath but George Dermody and Betsy Heidenbach. (She finally got him.) We call them The Lovers. They think they're hot shit because they're all over each other's bodies all the time. They can't even stand to go to classes apart from each other. You're always bumping into them in stairwells and corners and bushes. When I pulled the hay up off them, I sort of got the same feeling you get when you turn over a big rock and you see all these white wormy things kind of shrinking away. Like, "What's *that* doing here?"

A couple times I think I heard Debbie Breen screaming.

Finally the wagons stopped and we all got off and there was this big campfire waiting. Some of the parents were there throwing wood on it, and others were waving for us to come and make a circle around it and handing out these long sticks with points on and hotdogs. I don't know how it happened — I didn't pray for it, I never have good luck, and I don't believe in miracles for teenagers — but there I am along with everybody else, sticking my hotdog into the fire, and all of a sudden there's this voice right next to me: "Oh, it's too hot! My face is *burning!*"

One guess who the voice belonged to.

Not only that, but I just happened to be scrunched right up next to her. Shoulder to shoulder. Next thing I know — it's like I'm dreaming it — I'm grabbing her stick and saying, "Here, I'll take it. I'll bring it to ya."

I was amazed at how easy she gave up her stick. She just sort of dropped back then, complaining about her face.

I called, "How do you want it done?"

"Medium," she called.

Medium . . . the first word Debbie Breen ever spoke to me.

I didn't care too much about mine, but I babied that hotdog of hers in that fire. I rolled it up and down the flames like I was painting it. That fire, it tried to snatch the hotdog, but I wouldn't let it. I just gave the fire a little sniff. I teased it. And when I was done I had the mediumest hotdog there ever was.

No trouble finding her again; that lemon-yellow jacket was brighter than the fire. "This okay?" I asked her.

She looked at it, turned it over. "Yeah. Good. Thanks."

"Well, here" — I handed the stick to her — "I'll get some rolls."

They had the rolls over in a big cardboard box. Sodas too. I got two sodas, two rolls.

She was in a different place when I came back. "Okay," I said. "Gotcha a soda, okay?"

"Uh-huh," she said. She flicked her head. She was always doing that to get the hair out of her eyes. I could watch her flick her head like that for ten years.

So I got to sit next to her and pass her stuff that was going around the circle. Like mustard and relish and pretzels and potato chips. When the mustard came around, instead of handing her the jar, I said, "Here. Hold out your hotdog. You want a lot?"

She held her hotdog back. "Is it yellow or brown spicy?"

"Yellow."

She held it out. "A lot."

I couldn't believe how nice she was being. I used to think it would be hard to get to know her. But it wasn't. It was easy.

I wound up getting her another hotdog. Then another. And each time, I went around the circle looking for the yellow mustard. She spent most of the time talking to her girlfriends on the other side of her. But I didn't care. I just wished time didn't pass and fires didn't die out and stomachs didn't get full, so I could serve her forever. Debbie Breen. The cheerleader. Beautiful. Flick-flick. *The* Debbie Breen! And me.

I guess it was around the end of the second hotdog when the boss parent, Mister Burger, started telling scary stories.

A lot of the guys laughed at first and kept making funny noises, but by the end of the first story all you could hear was Mister Burger's voice and the fire crackling.

The story was about this late room in some junior high school, and how every time a kid got sent to it he never came out again. Just disappeared. Well, this one kid saw what was happening. He was never late a day in his life, but he started to get nervouser and nervouser because no matter how early he came to school, he was always almost late. He came earlier and earlier, and the late bell kept ringing sooner and sooner.

Then one day it rang just as he was opening his homeroom door. He knew what was coming the next day. He better do something. So what he did was, he never left school that day. He snuck into a janitor's closet after his last class and stayed there till everybody left: the kids, the teachers, and finally even the janitors. The last light went out.

All night, all night he crouches and shivers in a corner of the closet. And all he can hear are the clocks, ticking away all over the school, in the dark . . . up on the second floor . . . down in the basement . . . in the gym . . . the library . . . the teachers' lounge . . . everywhere. There seemed to be hundreds of them. They got louder and louder. They seemed to be moving. And then . . . and then . . . they stop! All of a sudden, all at once, the clocks stop ticking. And the kid has the strangest feeling he knows why: they're *listening*. He stuffs a rag in his mouth to keep his teeth from chattering.

Then the clocks start up again. Same as before . . . *tick-tock tick-tock* . . . louder . . . louder. . . . The kid can't stand it anymore. He takes the rag and rips it in half and stuffs it in his ears so he can't hear the clocks.

Sometime during the night the kid dozes off, and next

thing he knows there's this faint ringing somewhere. He quick wakes up and yanks the rag from his ears. It's the late bell! He crashes out of the closet, tears down the empty hallways, up the empty stairs, praying the bell will keep ringing. But it stops just before he pushes in his homeroom door.

All the kids turn toward him. They're all the ones that had disappeared. Their faces seem strange. And something else is strange too. It's a sound. He listens — ticking. Lots of little faint tickings. It's the students. They're not breathing; they're ticking! And the homeroom teacher is giving him this eerie grin, and he points out the door and says, "Late room."

Well, that was just the first story. You could sort of feel the circle inching up closer to the fire, and you started to notice how cool the back of your neck was. You kind of wanted to look behind you, just to check. We were in a clearing, and almost all around us was this gigantic pumpkin patch. You could make out a few pumpkins in front, looking like basketballs somebody left. Then it was all dark.

Next Mister Burger told a story about this bloody hand that kept crawling around strangling people. Then one about the ghost of a snake. But we never got to hear the end of that one, because halfway through it some girl sitting on the other side of the circle lets out this ear-splitting scream. Everybody started to laugh at first, figuring she was just scared of the story. But then she sort of half sat up and screamed again and went, "Something's there!" Her eyes were glowing and she was staring over our heads to behind us.

I turned around. We all turned around. Nobody could see anything. Nothing we could be sure of, anyway. The firelight kind of flickered into the pumpkin patch, and sometimes it did almost look like things were moving.

"Oh God," Debbie goes. "Something *is* there." She was grabbing the arm of one of her girlfriends. "Annie. Annieeee..."

Mister Burger was standing. His face was calm and smiling. "Well," he goes, "looks like I really did it now. Now you're all seeing things." He starts across the circle. "If I'm ever going to finish the story I guess I'll have to go have a look, huh?"

Some of the girls start squealing. "Oh, Mister Burger! No!"

But he keeps on walking. He cuts through the circle next to where we are, and he's saying if any brave souls want to go along with him, they can. And Debbie Breen is biting her lip and staring out into the unknown darkness and she's scared, she is scared.

I stood up. "I'll go," I said.

Peter Kim got up too, and some other kid I didn't know. Into the pumpkin patch. It was weird. The ground got darker and darker with each step. Pretty soon we were bumping into pumpkins.

"Okay, fellas," Mister Burger said, sort of whispery. "Let's fan out a little bit. When I call your name out, just yell 'Okay.' Okay?"

"Okay," we said.

"Okay, now, let's see: you're Peter Kim, right? And you're the Gruber boy. Howie? And you're ... you're ..."

"Jason Herkimer."

"That's right. Jason. Hard to see. Okay, let's go."

I'd be lying if I said I wasn't scared. But it's the honest-to-God's truth that I wasn't *real* scared. That's because when I *did* start to get almost real scared I thought about Debbie back there, all trembling and biting her lip, and the scared kind of got pushed out of the way by mad.

I started thinking about all the things it could be — if it really *was* something. Like, it could be an animal. Or some kind of kids messing around. Or some guy. Some weirdo. Maybe one of those perverts or rapists just hanging around waiting for one of the girls to sort of drift away from the group. I pictured Debbie drifting away. I pictured this big dark form hulking behind her. "Come on," I said under my breath, "come on, come on . . ."

Mister Burger called our names out. Everybody said okay.

My eyes were getting a little used to the dark. I could see about two pumpkins in front of me. I was freezing, but the palms of my hands were mushy. My mouth was like wood. My swallow wouldn't work.

I thought I saw something right ahead of me. I stopped. Nothing moved. Nothing made a noise. But something was different.

I took a step forward. It was on the ground. Something about the ground a couple yards away was different. Another step. I couldn't make out any pumpkins at the spot, and the darkness there seemed a little different shade, and there was a kind of wavy, floppy shape to it. I knelt down slow. I knelt down very slow. I was feeling for a stick and still keeping my eyes on it when all of a sudden there's this sharp *fsssss-thp* of air, like a tire inflating, and the damn thing is *moving!*

And *hissing!*

I turn, take off, and trip over a pumpkin, fall on my face, look back — it's *growing!* — get up and haul ass outta there. I'm almost back into the firelight when two things happen:

(1) I hear Mister Burger calling my name, (2) I remember Debbie Breen. I stop, pick up the only thing around, which is a pumpkin, and start heading back.

"Jason!" Mister Burger is calling.

I call back, "I got it!"

"Jason, got what? You okay?"

"I got it!"

"Jason!"

"I got it!"

I got it all right. By the time I got back, the thing was as high as a football goalpost. It was hissing and kind of swaying back and forth. A hundred hearts were thumping inside of me and every one of them was ready to explode, and I figured that throwing that pumpkin might be the last thing I ever did, but I was going to do it if it killed me.

Which I did. The pumpkin hit the thing, sort of towards the bottom. There was a clank and a louder-than-ever hiss and the thing just took off. It shot up into the air and curlicued and darted all over the place and all the time sounded like a dinosaur farting. Finally it plopped back down to earth, and that's when I heard laughing. A couple of people — parent-type people — were standing just behind where the thing used to be, and they were howling their heads off.

I asked them what it was. A dragon balloon, they said. And it still had some more growing to do when I hit the compressed air can. We went over to where it was, this big deflated flopdop of rubber. You had to look at it pretty long before you could tell it was a dragon.

By this time Mister Burger and the two other guys were with us. The parents told them what happened, and they were all having a good laugh. Everybody but me, that is.

We picked up the balloon and started carrying it, just like it was a real dead dragon carcass. There was a lot of commotion by now back at the fire. They were all standing at the edge of the firelight, staring. As we got closer and I could smell hotdog and mustard in the air and I could make out a patch of lemon-yellow jacket, I wanted to drop my end of the dragon and go hide in the pumpkins.

When everybody got back in a circle and quieted down, Mister Burger opened his big mouth and started telling them all what happened. But he didn't tell it the way I thought he would. Or even the way *I* would have told it.

He started off saying what the plan was. How the parents got this dragon balloon and hid with it out in the pumpkin patch. And how they let in this one girl on the secret, and told her to scream that she saw something out there. And how Mister Burger knew he could get at least a couple kids to go along with him.

"And everything was going along perfectly," said Mister Burger, "until Jason Herkimer messed it all up."

Everybody laughed. My face was hot from more than the fire.

"That's right, that's right," Mister Burger told on, "Jason Herkimer did not cooperate. What the plan called for was that whoever came across the dragon would be scared silly — and Jason *was* scared silly —"

Laughter.

"— and that the kid would take off and run like mad back to the fire."

Double laughter.

Mister Burger waited. "The rest of the plan called for everybody getting excited and scared around the fire, and then watching as the dragon comes looooming out of the darkness."

A little laughter, some ghost hoots.

"But we never got to that part of the plan. Why? Because Jason Herkimer turned around and went back. Why, I don't know. But apparently there was something in him that was bigger than being scared silly. And that something made him charge back into that dragon and kill it — with a pumpkin!"

Thundering laughs. Even I had to.

When Mister Burger started again, his voice was low. "The point is, my friends, that *we* knew it was all a joke. He did not." He took a step forward and looked right at me. "Jason Herkimer — Saint Jason" — he held up the drooping dragon — "well done, lad. You slew the dragon."

Then there was this dead silence for about a year. Everybody staring at me. Me staring at the dirt.

Then Dugan slapped me on the back. "Hey! Saint Jason!"

And then everybody started laughing and clapping and slapping palms. "Saint Jason! Saint Jason!" I kept hearing. Then they broke out the marshmallows, and somebody gave me a stick with one on it and said, "Here ya go, Saint. Here's your sword."

So all this stuff was going on and I was toasting my marshmallow — burning it actually, I like them black — when I hear, "Do you do marshmallows as good as you do hotdogs?"

Heaven. That's where I spent the rest of the night.

She talked to me:

"Aren't you the one that was wearing the patch on your eye?"

"How did you get hurt?"

"Oh neat! What position did you play?"

"Oh neat! Do you have any hobbies?"

"Oh neat! Can I see it sometime?"

And I talked to her:

"Yeah, that was me."

"Playin' football."

"Linebacker. But I'm going out for halfback next year."

"I'm making my own space station."

"Sure!"

I don't know how many marshmallows we had that night. I only know we were still doing them while they were putting out the fire and loading up the wagons for the ride back. (The Lovers were still in the hay. They never left.)

The way I did it, I would put both our marshmallows right on the same stick, right up next to each other. Touching. Then into the fire. (She likes hers black too.) And I do mean *into* the fire, right into the middle, so when you pull them out you have this flaming marshmallow torch. The flame is a little bit orange but mostly blue, and the white skin turns to brown and then black, crinkly-flaky, like ashes, which it is mostly, I guess. Then I would swing them around to cool them off (but not too much) and then we would take them off the stick. I'd let her go first. And the thing was, they wouldn't come apart too easy. Because they had sort of melted together, and when she tried to pull hers off, some of mine would come along with it.

Each time I would say, "Hey, you got some of mine there."

And she would say, "I don't care."

And then you pop the whole thing into your mouth, and your teeth crush through the black crusty part and sink into the soft white warm inside.

For the ride back she got into my wagon.

HALLOWEEN

THE NEXT NIGHT WAS HALLOWEEN. WE ALL DECIDED IT WOULD be the last year we got dressed up. We spent the day making phone calls: "What're you gonna wear?" "What're *you* gonna wear?"

I couldn't put my finger on it, but for me there still was something a little bit funny, or strange, or, I don't know, about Calvin Lemaine and Peter Kim talking about what they were going to dress up as. I mean, I remember one Halloween when I found this coolie hat and a pair of those fake buckteeth up in the attic, and I thought maybe I would go around as a Chinese. (So happens my mother didn't let me.) But what I mean is, until I got to know Peter pretty well, I always thought of Chinese (which is like Korean, which is what Peter Kim is) as something to be dressed up *as*.

Sort of the same thing with Calvin, him being black. Like, why did they ask me what they ought to be? They already *were* something.

Anyway, it was just at first that it seemed kind of funny.

Everybody met at my house. Calvin came as a bone. He

wore this white suit, like a chef or a hospital person wears. He didn't look any more like a bone than me.

I asked him what kind of bone he was supposed to be.

"Femur," he sniffs, like it was supposed to be obvious. "Thigh bone to you. Biggest bone of all."

Then he puts this sort of round knobby thing on his head, stands real straight, and puts his hands in his pockets.

"See?" he says.

He still didn't look like a bone.

The reason Calvin came as a bone is because he wants to become a doctor. He can tell you the names of every bone in your body. And just about everything else too.

Last year he was a ligament.

Peter Kim came as a football player. Really original, huh?

But the bad thing was, he had to bring his little brother along, Kippy Kim. Kippy's only four. That was bad for all of us, because the kid would slow us down and would want to go places we didn't and just be an all-around pain in the butt. None of us really liked him, because he was always insisting on going places with Peter, and his mother almost always made Peter take him along. We tried to dump him onto Cootyhead, who was going to take Timmy around, but Kippy screamed and said he would tell his mother if Peter dumped him.

But that was only half of it. The crazy, absolutely insane part was what he was dressed up as: Fu Manchu! He had the whole getup, including this evil-looking mask with the long droopy mustache. And the insanest thing of all was, sitting on top of the Fu Manchu mask was his Phillies baseball cap. Peter used to tell me he wore it all the time, even to bed sometimes, but until now I didn't believe him.

I didn't want to hurt Peter's feelings, so I dragged Dugan into the kitchen to laugh about it. We kept saying imagine what was going to happen when he goes up to some house, and they can't guess him, and so he takes off his Oriental mask and what's left? A little Oriental face! They'd have to laugh at him, but for all I cared it would serve him right for making such an ass out of himself. But what really surprised me was his family letting him get away with it.

Then Peter came in. "What's so funny?" he goes, as if he didn't know.

So we told him. He looked all bewildered.

"C'mon, Peter," I said. "Stop acting dumb."

"Who's acting? I still don't get it."

I took a deep breath. "Okay, look. I'll explain it, okay?" I went through it real slow, how ludicrous it was to wear this Oriental mask over an Oriental face.

"So?" he goes, *still* acting dumb.

I was losing my patience. "So? So? Look, Peter, this is Halloween, y'know? Halloween? Ever hear of it? United States of America? The whole idea is, you wear a mask to look like something else, something different."

"Fu Manchu *is* different."

"You know what I mean."

"No, I don't know what you mean." Peter's voice was squeaking now. "Fu Manchu is Chinese."

"Well?"

"Well, Kippy is American. Isn't that different enough?"

"Peter, look, that's not the point." And then all of a sudden I saw it was me who was missing the point. Peter probably did see how funny it was, but he figured it was more important to stick up for his kid brother. I could understand that. Korean families are very close. "Okay, okay, I see," I told him, and I passed around a bag of pretzels to get us off the subject.

Dugan came as himself, except for this dopey mask that he must have picked out of a garbage can on the way over. It didn't even have a rubber band on it; he just held it up to his face. Naturally he had his green-and-gold St. Stevie's jacket on. And his tie. His tie is like Kippy's cap: he wears it everywhere, not just to school. Wore it on the hayride. He's had this same tie since fourth grade. Only time he takes it off is when school lets out for the summer. Funny thing, though: it never makes him look dressed up.

But that's Dugan. He's always, well . . . Dugan. He just fits in everywhere. He just shows up. Wherever you are (if there's at least two of you), just turn around — there's Dugan. I think his tombstone will say:

Here lies Dugan
He showed up

Richie was a bum. Every year he's a bum. He always talks about these fantastic things he's going to be. But he can never find costumes for them in a store. And his mother never feels like taking half a year to make them. So all Richie ever actually does is make all these drawings and talk about it all year, and in the end he goes back to being a bum. He wears this ratty old black mothholey suit his father gave him, and this old pair of pointy roach-killer shoes with the little holes in them. And this cigar he has to promise not to light up.

Me, I was Luke Skywalker, from *Star Wars*. I knew all along I wanted to be something from space. I thought about being The Alien for a while, but that would be too hard. Then I had a brilliant idea: a black hole! But I couldn't figure out how to do it. I'm not like Calvin — I want to look real. (Plus if I was a black hole I didn't know what I would say to Calvin when he would ask me what I was.)

That brought me to *Star Wars*. I knew right away I didn't want to be cute, like the robots. Or weird or funny. That left out Chewbacca and the freaks in the bar. So it kind of came down to either Darth Vader or Luke Skywalker. I didn't know which one it would be until the night before, at the hayride, when Debbie Breen said she was going to go around as Princes Leia. I didn't tell her, but I knew right then it was going to be Skywalker.

I was cool. Pants tucked into a pair of my mother's boots. Blousy sleeves. Timmy's toy sword (he steals my dinosaurs) that I painted green, the blade of. Lone Ranger mask. I was cool.

So out we go, Kippy and all. Of course, everybody else was only worried about getting their bags filled and where to get the best stuff. But my mind wasn't on candy. My mind was on steering everybody over to Debbie Breen's neighborhood, which was about ten blocks away. So I kind of got us started in that direction, and then when somebody wanted to hang a right or left I would jump in real quick and say, "Hey, look, right ahead, I got *two* peanut butter cups there last year!" Or, "Why you want the same old places? All we ever get's apples and crackers every year."

When I ran out of those reasons I pulled out the big gun: "Okay, you guys wanna go back, go ahead. I'm goin' this way." Which worked, because on Halloween almost anybody will give in to somebody who knows where you can get good stuff. Or says he knows.

Lucky for me, we kept getting just enough good stuff so there wasn't a mutiny. The closer we got to Debbie's neighborhood, the more Richie kept giving me this grin in back of his cigar.

Naturally nobody guessed us after a while, because we weren't in any of our neighborhoods. Actually, Kippy came in kind of handy. Some of us, especially me and Calvin, were a little shy about going up to all these strange houses. But Kippy didn't care. Uh-uh. He just tore from one house to the next. He learned houses with lights on meant people with treats, so he was always yelling, "Yight! Yight!" (He talks funny because he can't say some letters.)

So we would let him knock on the doors and sort of soften the people up. The usual scene went something like this: Kippy bangs on door. Lady opens. Kippy says, "Fwick or fweet, mell my feet." Lady says, "Oh look, Lester. I believe we have Fu Manchu here. Apparently he's been signed up by the Phillies. Come on in, Mister Manchu." Lady looks up and sees us. Half the smile goes away, but she says, "Come on, boys." They try and try and try to guess Kippy Kim, who's so dumb he thinks they ought to know him, so he keeps shaking his head and saying, "Nope. Geh again." At long last (there's other Halloweeners bunching up at the door by now), he takes the mask off, and the lady gets this funny look and says, "Well, well. And what is your name?" (Me and Dugan keep waiting for one of the ladies to go, "Well, glory be, Lester! Look here: a Chinababy!" But they never do.)

Meanwhile, almost as funny as that, The Bone is standing there at attention the whole time. And Dugan is getting tireder and tireder of holding his mask up; his hand slips until all it's covering is about one eyeball. If I wasn't so anxious to get to Debbie Breen's neighborhood, I would have thought the whole thing was hilarious. But I could have killed Kippy Kim for making the people guess so long.

When we got five blocks from her house I started looking for Princess Leia. The fifth block went. The fourth block. The place was crawling with Darth Vaders and Artoo Detoos. Even a Chewbacca. But no Princess Leia.

The third block. The closer we got the scareder I got. I was afraid we'd miss her — and afraid we wouldn't miss her. I wondered how it would be. Would she go around with all of us? Or would just us two go off together? I could picture the guys hooting at us. Dugan's whistle. We wouldn't care. We'd just laugh and go from house to house . . . *"Oh look, Lester — Princess Leia and Luke Skywalker!"* . . . candy flowing into our open bags . . . trading favorites . . . the best part between houses, because we're holding our bags on the outside because on the inside we're holding hands. . . .

Then I saw her, the Princess, coming down from a lighted porch and ready to turn up the sidewalk toward us.

I grabbed Kippy and half shoved him across the street. "Hey, c'mon, you guys," I called. "Over here. This looks like a great one." They grumbled but they came.

When we walked up to the house on the other side of the street I was shaking like a leaf. There was an empty space where my stomach used to be. I didn't dare look back. I was only glad I hadn't told her who I was going to be. And I was glad I hadn't told the guys who she was going to be. So I was the only one who knew Debbie Breen was out Halloweening with another Luke Skywalker.

TROUBLE

I GOT SENT HOME FROM SCHOOL TODAY. WITH A NOTE. FROM the vice-principal. (You always know it's princi-*pal* instead of princi-*ple* because the princi*pal* is your *pal*. Right? Right.) It says I have to bring a parent along for a meeting with him tomorrow morning.

Until then I'm not allowed to go inside that school. Not even if I *wanted* to. They would stop me. What it means is, I'm suspended.

I was never suspended from school a day in my life. I was never even late, unless I had a note. Suspended. Me. I can't get over it.

I'm a criminal.

I guess it all started with the first warning. (Three warnings and you're suspended.) No. I guess you'd have to say it started with Ralphie Smitht. Ralphie is famous, sort of. There are only four families in the United States that spell Smith Smitht, with a *t* on the end. You say it the same way. The *t*, the second *t*, is silent. Every time Ralphie goes to a new grade we always kind of sit there and grin because we know exactly what the teacher going to say. First she's going to think there was a mistake and ask him to say his name. Then, when she hears it, her face will screw up and she'll squint back into the roll book, look back at Ralphie and go, "With a *t*?"

Maybe it was the *t* on the end of his name that made Ralphie Smitht the way he is. He's always laughing. Like the *t* stands for tickle. I mean always. Even at nothing. Even at sad stuff. Once at a varsity football game he was laughing because we were losing, and this ninth-grader kept telling Ralphie to knock it off. But the more he said it, the more Ralphie laughed. So the kid pushes Ralphie off the top of the stands. When I got down to the ground, there he was, laughing.

Now the thing about Ralphie Smitht: he doesn't like to laugh alone. He's always trying to catch your eye or pull on your sleeve or hit you with a spitball to get your attention. It is very, very hard not to laugh along with somebody like that. Like trying not to sneeze with pepper all over the place. And if you finally do break down and start laughing along with him, it's even harder not to do it the next time. In other words, it gets easier and easier to laugh.

And the final thing I'm saying, like where there's smoke there's fire: where there's all that laughing, there's trouble.

Well, I've been holding out against Ralphie Smitht ever since fourth grade. Not that I never-ever laughed, but I never really caved in. Maybe once a month he would finally get to me, and this giggle would pop out of my mouth. But I always tried to hide it. I didn't want to give him the satisfaction. Because actually, I thought he was an idiot nurd jackass and I couldn't stand him.

Then the week after Halloween, after all those years, I caved in.

It happened in science class. The lights were out and the shades were down because we were having a movie. It was about gravity. It started off showing Isaac Newton being plunked on the head by an apple. That got Ralphie started. Then the movie, which was like a cartoon, started showing all these other things falling all over the place: raindrops, leaves, meteors, baseballs, chicken eggs, kids on sliding boards, broken balloons. Every time something came down, Ralphie would laugh a little harder. And the next thing I knew I was laughing too. Cracking up. Roaring.

We started dropping stuff onto the floor to go along with the movie. Then we started making our own drop sounds, all kinds of *splats, ploops, buhbumbuhs, frrrgles*. And pretty soon they weren't even dropping noises. Just noises. Just about every kind of fart noise you can think of. Ralphie let out a really good mouth-fart, and then followed it up with a great belch. (He can bring up a belch whenever he wants; along with the final *t*, he's famous for that too.) Well, my answer was one of those cracklers you do by putting your hand in your armpit and mashing down hard and fast with your arm. I ripped a super one that almost blew Ralphie off his seat. I was getting ready for the next one when all of a sudden the lights go on. The teacher is glaring straight at me. And there I am: my shirt unbuttoned, my hand sticking into my armpit, and my elbow up over my head.

A couple minutes later I was in the vice-principal's office. Warning Number 1.

I didn't stand a chance after that. After all those years Ralphie Smitht finally had me, and no way he was going to let me go. I was putty in his mouth.

We would pass in the halls and just crack up at the sight of each other. In fact, it got so I didn't even have to see him.

Once I was just walking along innocently with Richie when all of a sudden, from down the hallway and around the corner, I hear this moosecall. I didn't even think. I just moosecalled back.

"Man, you're gone crazy," Richie said.

Maybe I was. Thinking back on it, it's like a dream. Mostly what I remember is a lot of laughing and moose-calling and funny noises and just plain crazy, crazy stuff. The trouble was I kept waking up in the vice-principal's office.

The last thing they got me for was the talent show assembly. Every year they let the kids that want to get up on the stage and perform, like sing and stuff. So me and Ralphie manage to sit together during the show, and we're having a great old time snickering at the acts and booing at the end when everybody else is clapping.

Except when Debbie Breen came on. She got together with some of the other cheerleaders and good-looking girls and did this song-and-dance thing that they wore pajamas for. Debbie wore these real short baby-doll jobs. Pink. She just kept smiling the whole time she danced and sang, flicking her head, so beautiful. I tried to laugh along with Ralphie, but I just couldn't. I couldn't boo or clap at the end.

Then onto the stage comes this tall skinny girl, all by herself — and she's playing a trombone! Talk about laughing. Half the audience beat me and Ralphie to the punch. You could hardly hear the trombone.

All of a sudden I knew what I had to do. I signaled to the teacher at the end of the row that I had to go to the lavatory. Okay, she said. I got up. Out to the aisle. Up to the back of the auditorium. I stop just outside one of the doorways. Look up and down the hallway. Nobody there. The lavatory's right across the way. I peek back into the auditorium. The only one facing me is that fool tromboner on the stage. The rest is just backs of heads. Row after row of backs of heads. The whole school . . .

I do it. I cup my hands right toward the trombone and give a moosecall so loud I can't believe it came from me. It all happened so fast, not a head moved by the time I ran. (My feet were already pointed toward the lavatory.) But as the lavatory door was swinging shut behind me, I could hear them roaring in the auditorium.

I didn't really have to go, but I figured a stall was the best place to be. I went in one — one with a good latch — and closed it and sat down. I was shaking. My heart was pounding. I was sweating all over.

I heard the lavatory door creak open. Steps. Shoes outside my stall. Adult's. I gave some good grunts, but the shoes didn't move. A knock on the stall door, inches from my nose.

"Somebody in here," I said.

"Open, please," the voice said.

I reached forward and slid the latch over. The door swung open. It was the vice-principal.

PUNISHMENT

My mother looked up from the suspension note. "Jason, what's gotten *into* you?"

I shrugged. "Nothin'." I tried to look nonchalant and normal, but I don't think I made it. It's hard to look normal when you're sitting in your living room at eleven-thirty on a school-day morning, and you're not sick.

"Nothing?" she goes. "You were suspended for nothing?"

"I don't know."

"Well, what is it that you did? What could you have possibly done to get suspended?"

"I don't know. Nothin'. Stuff."

She squinted at me. "Stuff?" She looked at the ceiling. "Stuff?" She looked at me. "What stuff?"

I was *not* going to tell her. "I don't know," I said. "I was laughing. That's all."

I thought my mother would get mad and yell. But she didn't. She only looked surprised. And confused. "I don't understand it," she kept saying. "This isn't like you, Jason. Ham's not going to believe it."

But Ham did believe it. When he came home and my mother showed him the note, all he said was, "So?"

Now my mother was double confused. "He's suspended," she said.

Ham's lower lip jutted out. He nodded. "So I see." Then he started up the stairs.

"Wait," my mother said. "Isn't this serious?"

Ham laid a hand on the banister. "Well, yes and no. It's serious as far as the school is concerned. And maybe as far as you're concerned. But from a cosmic point of view, this is just another teenager going mad." He pointed. "Look at Jason." They both looked at me in the corner reclining chair. "He's not bothered. He's got the cosmic point of view."

My mother came back with a good one. "Well, where's your cosmic point of view," she asked him, "when you're getting an ulcer over him taking your food out of the refrigerator?"

Ham just smiled and wagged his hand. "So? The food directly affects me. This doesn't. I reserve the right to get angry when my food disappears."

"But you're not bothered about this. This is not important enough for you to be bothered about."

Ham leaned on the banister with both hands, looked at me, looked at my mother. "Honey, to tell you the truth, after I've been thinking about this for a while and we've been talking about it, yes, it probably will start to bother me. In fact, I can almost guarantee it. It's just that right now, right this minute, I've just walked into the house after teaching all day, and I'm told Jason's been suspended from school, and I'm trying not to treat it like it's the end of the world. I'm trying to enjoy my indifference while it lasts."

Just then Cootyhead comes into the house, and right away she sees I'm in trouble. So she plops down onto the sofa and pretends to be interested in some magazine.

"Get her outta here!" I holler. "Get her outta here!"

Ham tells her, "Out, Mary. Out or upstairs."

Cootyhead says what's the matter, she's just looking at a magazine.

"Mary."

"But I have to find pictures of water for school."

"Mary."

She goes upstairs, but no door shuts.

"Mary. Door."

The door shuts.

Mom says, "It's not like him, Ham."

Ham held up a finger. "Not like he *was*. But that's not to say it's not like he *is*." You have to be a genius to follow what he's saying sometimes. "Remember what happened recently."

"What's that?"

"His birthday. Even you were kidding him about becoming a teenager."

"Jason is still Jason."

Ham shut his eyes and wagged his head. "No, no, dear. Jason is not Jason. Not completely. Not anymore. Never again. What we see sitting there in that chair is but a remnant of the Jason we once knew. In fact the pronoun *he* is hardly suitable anymore. It is just an abandoned skin we see there. The shell of the cicada. Perfect in every detail. Even the eye sockets. But go over there, turn him over, go ahead" — (she didn't) — "turn him over and you'll see the crack between the shoulder blades. There, where the worm is struggling to get out. The thirteen-year-old does not change from a worm to a butterfly, you know. It changes from a butterfly to a worm."

He's saying all this without cracking a smile, like he always does. Real dramatic too. Arms moving around. Eyes going wide open, then scrunching down. Like he was in that amateur theater. "Or if you want to put it more geologically," he goes, "what we have sitting over there is a fossil."

My mother said, "You're a big help," and headed for the kitchen.

Ham reached out. "No, wait, honey. I'm only half kidding. Really. Don't worry. I'll go over to the school with him. I'll talk to the vice-principal. But I'm just saying, a lot of it has to do with his age. That's all."

My mother glanced at me before turning to Ham. Her eyes were shining. "That's easy for *you* to say."

Ham came down. "Jason, go upstairs now. Okay?"

He meant into my room, but I just went up and hung around the top of the steps. I stuck my ear through the banister posts. I could just about hear them in the kitchen.

"Honey, people have always told us, right? 'Wait'll you have your first teenager, wait'll you have your first teenager.'"

"Yes, I know. But I can't believe you're going to be so blasé about it when it's Timmy's turn."

By that my mom meant that Timmy is *his* kid. His *real* kid.

"Honey, I can't deny certain things. Blood is blood. I can't—"

"I understand that."

"No, listen to what I'm saying—"

"I do. I understand."

"You're not listening. Now listen. So. Maybe there is something there with — uh" — I couldn't make out the next word — "that can't be duplicated. But that doesn't mean I don't care."

"I know that."

"No, you don't. I mean more than just care. I mean, you live in the same house with a couple of kids for, what, four years now, and you wrestle with them in their pajamas" (I don't do that anymore) "well, they come to mean more to you than just a couple kids down the block. You know?"

"I know. I know."

"But?"

"You didn't exactly seem devastated about Jason hurting his eye at that football game. You seemed more interested in whether the school would pay for it."

"I'm sorry."

"Okay, okay."

"Honey, what do you want?"

"Oh, I don't know. I guess I would like for someday you to say you love my kids."

"Who says I don't?"

"You don't say you do."

"Hey, are you complaining about how I treat you, or the kids?"

"See? Always joking."

"Honey, don't trust my reactions. Not the first, flip ones anyway. You know me. I'm not obvious. I'm an actor — remember? Believe me, it bothered me when Jason got kicked in the eye. I wasn't happy. Honest."

"So . . . the suspension?"

"Look, you're right. If Timmy gets suspended from school

in seventh grade, I'll probably be upset. Maybe more than I am now. But I'll tell you one thing. If it does happen, I'm going to try my damnedest to remember one thing."

"What's that?"

"That he's not just a teenager. He's a *junior high school* teenager. I would never teach in junior high school. I've seen them. That's why I teach in college. I'm telling you, they're different creatures."

"Shall we have him as a pet instead of a son, then? Make up a box in the cellar for him to sleep in?"

"May be. May be. I'm telling you, the Jason we knew is being pushed out of his skin. It is the time of the new monster. Even he doesn't know what's going on."

Then this banshee screeching behind me: "Mommeee! He's listening! He's listening!"

I was in my room before I was told. Ham was right. I couldn't understand all those words, but it sounded like he was saying stuff that I was already thinking about myself. Like something weird going on inside of me. It seemed like all during that week there were two me's. The one me kept laughing and messing around with Ralphie Smitht and getting into trouble. That me just seemed to go off on its own. I couldn't even keep track of it. And then every day I would catch up with it in the vice-principal's office.

But the other me, that's the one I was really paying attention to. And that other me was only interested in one thing: *Who was the other Luke Skywalker?*

I had to be cool. I couldn't let on to the guys what happened. But I asked around and dropped hints and talked about Halloween and talked about *Star Wars*. Zero. Zip. I still couldn't find out who it was. I only knew what I saw myself: he looked pretty tall. All the time Debbie Breen was on the stage in her pink PJ's I kept wondering: *Is he somewhere in here watching her too?*

Next morning Ham went with me to school. It was embarrassing. I tried to stay ahead of him, but he kept calling, "Hey, wait up there, old boy."

The vice-principal didn't look too mad. He had my records there, and he said what a good student I always was back to the first grade, and never any discipline problem. He said the teachers were all surprised at my behavior. But he was sure I was just getting something out of my system.

Then he got up and said, "Be right with you," and walked out. I figured that was going to be it. But in a minute he comes walking back with — guess who — the girl with the trombone. *Oh shit,* I thought.

The two of them just sort of stood there in the middle of the room. The vice-principal was smiling. Ham stood up. I stood up.

"Jason," the vice-principal said, still smiling, "this is Marceline McAllister."

I nodded. I think I grunted. Up close, I recognized her from being in the other academic section. She didn't say anything. She didn't nod back. She didn't smile.

"Jason, I guess you know Marceline, don't you?"

"Not really," I said.

"Well, you recognize her." He chuckled a little and glanced at Ham. "You've seen her before someplace, haven't you?"

"Yeah, I guess."

She was glaring straight at me. Down actually, since she

was taller. Like a boxer in the middle of the ring before a fight.

"Don't you have something to say to Marceline, Jason?"

What would I possibly have to say to her? "I do?" I said.

I looked around. All three were staring at me. Eyes and silence. Then it hit me. *Oh shit.*

"Jason."

"Uh" — I gulped — "I'm sorry."

"Jason, she's not lying on the rug."

I looked up, up, into those stone eyes. "I'm sorry."

The stone face cracked. It spoke. "I hope so." She turned and went.

"She's an excellent musician," the vice-principal told Ham. "A member of the district band."

As soon as it was okay I got out of there. The last thing I heard was Ham behind me, saying to the vice-principal, "He's a good kid. He really is."

Was he acting?

PIMPLES

I NOTICED IT FOR THE FIRST TIME YESTERDAY MORNING. IN THE bathroom. I was taking a pee at the time and just sort of leaning over into the mirror — and there it was. I was so shocked I lost my balance, and I had to clean up the floor a little.

It was on my chin. A little bit right of center. It's funny how I knew it was a pimple the instant I saw it. I mean, why didn't it occur to me it could be a measle? Or cancer? Anything else. But no, I just knew it. Without even thinking. Teenage instinct, I guess.

It was ugly and red and smooth and gleaming and swollen and about the size of a small mountain. I touched the end of it with my fingertips. I almost got the shakes. It was like touching a roach.

I felt around it. Pressed. It hurt a little. It was in there, all right. Rooted in my face.

I went down for breakfast. I took two bites of toast and came back up. It was still there. It was saying: "I am all yours, bay-beee."

And it looked even bigger. It was growing!

No way I was going to school.

But I had to. Big test in math.

I snuck into my mother's compact. I put some powder on it. Wouldn't fool anybody. I put a Band-Aid on it, a little round one.

After each class I went to a boys' room. It was getting worse. Redder. Harder. Bigger. Uglier. It was pushing out the Band-Aid. Pretty soon it would look like a zit wearing a sombrero.

For lunch I stayed away from everything that looked like it might have oil or sweet stuff in it. Which was just about everything. I had celery and water.

When I checked in the mirror before the last period of the day I almost screamed. It had a yellow head. It was hideous. It was out of control. I was doomed.

I squeezed it. It shot out like a yellow bullet. I could *hear* it splat. If a bug was walking in the line of fire right at that moment, it would have been killed.

I kept squeezing until all the yellow was gone. Then a kind of pale watery stuff. Then pink. I didn't stop until there was nothing but good, solid, deep red blood coming out.

I couldn't believe it — if anything, the pimple looked bigger!

I was starting to see why modern man, who flew to the moon, could not conquer the pimple.

The sticky was gone from the Band-Aid, so I threw it away. Somehow I got through the last class and out of school. I didn't take the bus. I walked home. Alone. For once I wished I carried a handkerchief, so I could hold it in front of my chin.

The only thing good about the day, if you want to call it good, was that Debbie Breen didn't see me. I went different routes so I wouldn't pass her. The bad thing was, this was the day I was going to ask her about coming over to see my space station. She didn't say anything about it since the hayride, but that was okay because I needed a little time to finish up a real neat part. Now, I keep having this picture in my mind of her seeing me. She takes one look at the zit and practically vomits. Girls like Debbie Breen don't have to settle for zit-faces.

And speaking of faces — that's the cruelest part of all: they're on your face. I mean, do they *have* to be there? Why not on your feet? Your stomach? Your butt? I'd trade one on my face for a hundred on my butt.

After school I went to the drugstore. I took all my bagging money, and I bought things that say they will scrub it away ("with thousands of tiny scrubbers" — that sounded good), starve it, dry it up, kill it, zap it (Zap-A-Zit), and hide it.

I went home and tried them all. I even mixed them.

At dinner my mother noticed the Band-Aid. So did Ham. "Cut yourself shaving there, ol' boy?" he says.

"Hah!" goes Cootyhead. "He has a *pim-pul*." She spit out the *p*'s.

I tried to explain that I cut myself in woodshop.

We had chicken for dinner. I asked for hot tea too, which surprised my mother.

When we were about done, Ham says, "Anybody want more chicken?" He was looking at me under his eyebrows. Nobody said anything. "Okay," he goes, and he dumps the chicken — it's a breast — into a Baggie and puts it in the refrigerator. "That . . . will be my lunch tomorrow. My Lunch."

I asked if it was okay to take my tea upstairs. In the bathroom I took the boiling hot teabag and put it on the pimple. Just made it redder.

Then I went to the library. I asked the librarian if they had any medical books. She gave me these big huge jobs. I was looking for "acne" and "pimple" and "zit," but all I could find was "appendicitis" and "birth canal" and stuff like that.

So I looked around myself and I came up with this ratty old thing with a squashed bug inside it called *Old World Folklore and Home Art Remedies*. I looked in the boils and warts section and hit paydirt: a small paragraph on pimples. It said pimples were a sign of the Devil in adolescents, and the only way to get rid of them was to squeeze some pus onto — oh no! — the bone of a chicken. Then you wrap it in cloth worn by a virgin and bury it.

I hated to even think about it. But the more I looked at that sucker, and the more I thought of it being only the first of thousands more, and the more I thought of Debbie Breen, I knew what I had to do. I would never be able to live with myself if I ever found out later that the one thing I didn't try, no matter how crazy it sounded, really would have worked.

For the virgin's cloth I went up to the attic to the box where Cootyhead keeps her summer clothes. I got an old shirt of hers with birds on it.

As for the pus, I already squeezed it all out in school. I needed more. I ate some cake. A spoonful of jelly. A couple fingertips of raw sugar. I got down some cooking oil and dabbed the pimple with that. I smeared it with Crisco. I sat on my bed and worked up some dirty thoughts. I thought about every girl I knew, except Debbie. I thought about pubic hair and nipples and French kissing and The Lovers and fallopian tubes and ovaries and everything. I kept looking in the mirror. No yellow. Where was it when you needed it?

I thought about asking some ninth-grader for a donation. But I figured it had to be your own.

I went to bed but stayed awake. While I was lying there in the dark I made up a poem:

> Nothing is simple
> About a pimple

Everybody else went to bed. I waited. Pus or no pus, I was going to do it.

I snuck down to the kitchen and got the chicken. Some bone was showing. It was hard not to eat the meat. I squeezed a little blood bead onto my fingertip and rubbed it onto the bone. I wrapped it up good in the shirt and buried it in the yard, under the snowball plant.

I kept thinking about how a conversation between me and Ham would go:

> Ham: *Did you eat my chicken breast?*
> Me: *No.*
> Ham: *Did you take it?*
> Me: *Yes.*
> Ham: *But you didn't eat it?*
> Me: *No.*
> Ham: *Then what, pray tell, did you do with it?*
> Me: *I buried it.*

Before I went to bed I took one last look at the pimple. I didn't even have it twenty-four hours yet, but it seemed like a year. I knew that pimple better than I knew my nose.

What would it be like in the morning? Better? Worse? A second one?

I didn't care. I was exhausted. I went to sleep.

In the morning I woke up from a yell downstairs:

"MY CHICKENNNNN!"

GRANDMOTHERS

WE WERE IN LUNCH LINE AND PETER KIM WAS LOOKING IN HIS wallet for his lunch card. There was a picture of an old lady in his wallet. That seemed a little strange.

"Who's that?" I asked him.

"Who?"

"That. That old lady."

"That's my grandmother."

When we got to a table and sat down, I said, "Peter, is that something Koreans do a lot?"

"What?" he said.

"Carry their grandmothers' pictures in their wallets?"

Peter Kim never looks up when he eats. He really gets into his food. I thought of starving Chinese. I tried to picture him with chopsticks. So happens we were having this chicken stuff over rice.

"I keep" — he swallowed — "telling you. I don't know about Koreans."

That's true, he *is* always telling me that. But for some reason I just can't believe 100 percent of it. I look at his round tan face and those eyes that are spaced so far apart and almost flat with his forehead and as black as his hair and shaped like teardrops sideways, and I just can't believe he doesn't know any more about Koreans than me.

So we went into this little thing we always say:

"C'mon, you know you're a Korean."

"I am not a Korean."

"So what are ya?"

"I'm an American."

I said, "Okay now, serious. You gotta admit, most kids don't carry pictures of their *grand*mothers around in their wallet. You *gotta* admit that."

"I do?"

"Peter, come *on*. If I had a wallet, which I don't — and that's another thing: most guys don't even *have* wallets. Or at least they don't *use* them."

"Why not?" he goes.

"I don't know," I told him. "How do I know? Maybe because they don't have grandmothers' pictures to put *in* them. Anyway. What I'm saying is, like if *I* had a wallet, okay?"

"Okay."

"If I *had* a wallet, I wouldn't have my grandmother's picture in it."

"Why not?"

Getting this guy to see things sometimes . . . "I don't know. I just wouldn't."

"Who would you have a picture of?" he said.

"Oh, I don't know." I started thinking. My mother? Father? Ham? Timmy? "My bike, maybe," I said. "Or my space station."

For the first time he looked up. "You got a space station?"

"Yeah," I said. "I'm making it myself."

"Yeah? What's it like?" He was all excited.

I told him it was hard to describe. So why didn't he come over to my house after school.

He was impressed when he saw it. He wanted to know how big it was going to be. I told him I was just going to keep adding on to it, so it might be as big as my bed by the time it was finished. "Man!" he goes.

"This is nothin', what you see here," I told him. "This is just mostly the foundation. I don't even know what shape it's gonna be."

He pointed. "That's done, though. What is it? The solar antenna?"

I was surprised he would know that. "Yeah," I said. "That's it. I made it out of clothes hanger wire and aluminum foil."

"Neato."

"Yeah. What it does is, it collects the sun's rays to use them for heating water and to keep warm and stuff."

"Don't it change some of the rays into electricity? Like for lights?"

I said right, it does that too. "Listen," I said, "I didn't know you were all into space. When did you get interested?"

"I don't know," he said. "This okay?" He was turning the solar antenna.

I told him okay, I made it to turn. So it would always face the sun.

"I don't know," he said again. "I was just always interested in that stuff. The planets, y'know?"

"Stars."

"Yeah, stars. Red giants especially."

"Oh man, yeah! Some of them get so big they almost take up a whole solar system!"

"Black holes," he goes.

"Oh *man!* Peter, do you know" — I was really getting worked up now — "they're so strong, they suck in everything. Nothing can escape."

"Not even light."

"Not even light! Peter, imagine!"

We stared into each other's eyes for a while, me sitting on the bed, Peter at the space station, his hand on the solar antenna, trying to imagine.

A tiny grin slunk onto his face. "Quasars," he said.

"Aaiii!" I went and flopped backward onto the bed.

"Pulsars."

"Ahhhh!"

"Galaxies."

"Ouuuu!"

He was standing over me now. I was squirming, like I was the Devil and he was the Exorcist throwing holy water on me.

"Light-years. Comets. Asteroid belts. Space dust. Gamma rays. Alpha Centauri. The Big Bang."

Even Peter couldn't stand it anymore. He collapsed on the bed and we just laughed our heads off for about a year. This was great. I never saw Peter Kim talk so much. Or act like this.

Finally, when we were down to just sniffing and wiping our eyes, I said, "You forgot one thing."

"What's that?"

"*Pioneer.*"

He sort of swooned. "Ohhh yeahhh. *Pioneer.*"

"Do you ever think about it?" I asked him.

"Yeah," he goes.

"Out there?"

"Yeah."

We both thought about *Pioneer* for a while. Out there. Sailing through space. Farther and farther from earth. Carrying its gold plaque on board with the drawings of the nude man and lady. And other drawings and numbers and stuff. Just in case.

"Where's it supposed to be now?" I said. "You know?"

"I'm not sure. It passed Jupiter, didn't it?"

"Oh yeah. Long time ago."

"Saturn?"

"Yeah. I think so."

"What's next?"

"Uranus, ain't it?"

"Or Neptune."

"Yeah," I said, "maybe it *is* Neptune. I always forget about Neptune."

Peter sat up. "Yeah! I always forget about Neptune too. It's pretty big."

"I think so," I said, not very sure. "Is it the one that's all frozen ice?"

"Like dry ice?"

"Yeah."

"I don't know. Maybe that's Uranus."

We tried to figure it out. We couldn't.

"Well," I said, "I'll tell you one thing."

"What's that?"

"Know what really gets to me?"

"What?"

I closed my eyes, said it slow. "When I think . . . of *Pioneer* . . . going . . . out . . . past . . . Pluto. Know what I mean?"

"Yeah. I know."

"It passes Pluto . . . and it's *out* . . . of the Solar System. *Out* of it. Heading . . . heading . . ."

I looked at my arm. "Peter, look! My arm! See?"

They were there, all over my arm: goosebumps. "I toldja how I get. Do you get that way?"

"I don't know," he said. "I never looked."

"But you feel funny inside, don't you?"

"Yeah."

"Kinda like . . . fuzzy?"

"Yeah. Sort of."

"Dizzy almost?"

"Yeah."

"Bubbles?"

"Yeah!"

"Tiny cool little dizzy bubbles all over?"

"Yeah! Yeah!"

"I'll bet you get them too," I told him. "Let's see — what makes you feel the funniest?"

He thought awhile. "Mmm. Speed of light?"

"Okay," I said. "Speed of light. Coming up. One hundred and eighty-six thousand miles a second. A *second*. Got that?"

He nodded.

"Okay. Close your eyes."

He closed them.

"Okay, now. Speed of light." I smacked my dresser with my hand. Then again right away. "Hear that?" I said.

"Yep."

"That was a second. Right?"

"Right."

I did it again. "One second."

"One second."

"One second. One measly little second. One sixtieth of a minute; and in that measly little second, light can travel a hundred and eighty-six thousand miles. That's seven or eight times around the earth, man. Think about it."

I kept an eye on his arm. Nothing yet.

"One second. Imagine a car going that fast. A plane. The fastest plane. The fastest rocket even."

No bumps yet.

"Imagine. Imagine . . . getting on the rocket and going around the world seven times — *seven times* — and then getting off. And when you get off it's only one second later: *one . . . measly . . . second!*"

His arm was smooth as a baby's butt. "You sure you're trying?" I said. "Look."

He looked at the arm. "Yeah. I was thinking about it good."

"Didn't you feel anything start to sort of pop a little under your skin?"

He screwed his face up. "I don't know. It's hard to tell." He closed his eyes again and held his arm out. "Try distance this time."

We tried distance. I told him about how things are so far apart in the universe that even light, as fast as it goes, can take hundreds and thousands and even millions of years to get from one part of the universe to another.

Still no bumps.

We tried gamma rays, passing through steel like it was air.

Nothing. He was disappointed.

Time to bring in the heavy artillery.

"Only one left that could do it," I told him.

"What's that?"

"Infinity."

He shook his head, sort of smiled. "Forget it."

"Why?" I said.

"I *know* that one won't do anything."

"You *know*? How can you know? D'jever try it?"

"Sure. Just never bothered me."

I couldn't believe it: infinity. "You talkin' about the same infinity I am?" I asked him.

"Yep."

"Doesn't do anything to you?"

"Nope."

"No bubbles?"

"Nope."

"A little dizzy?"

"Nope."

This I couldn't believe. "You go out as far as you can, right?"

"Right."

"Out past the last quasar, right?"

"Right."

"Out past the last pulsar."

"Right."

"Past the last anything. *Anything*."

He nodded.

My mind took a deep breath. "You're going on and on . . . leave the galaxies behind . . . going at the speed of light . . . on and on . . . for years . . . thousands of light-years . . . *millions* . . ."

I was walking around in circles. My thoughts were getting

wispier and wispier, hard to hold on to, seeping out of my head, out through the cracks in my brain.

". . . *billions* of light-years. Sooner or later, sooner or later, you have to come to the end, right, Peter? You *have* to."

He just sat there.

"But if you come to the end — if there *is* an end — what comes *after* the end? *After* the end? Nothin'? Ever think about nothin', Peter? What's nothin'? Space? That's not nothin', right? All kinds of stuff in space. So what can there be at the end of space? Huh?"

His round face never moved.

"So I mean, if you can't imagine it coming to an end, maybe it doesn't end, huh? Maybe it just goes on forever and ever." I threw up my hands. "Great . . . swell . . . never ends. So how you supposed to imagine that either? So you don't even know how to think. You can't imagine it ending. And you can't imagine it not ending. Great."

I was sweating. Peter looked calm as the moon. "You gonna tell me that don't fuzz you up a little bit?" I said.

He shook his head sheepishly. He was right: not a bump in sight.

"Man!" I went. "My brain feels like somebody sprayed it with fizz just listening to myself. You mean you can think about all that and it doesn't bother you any more than a . . . a banana?"

He sighed. "I guess not."

"You don't feel anything."

"I didn't say that."

Aha! "So what do you feel?"

"Water," he said.

"*Water?* Whattaya mean? Drinking it? Swimming in it?"

"I don't know. Just water."

"Fishing?"

"I don't know."

"W-A-T-E-R water?"

"Yep."

Water. This kid was more complicated than I ever thought. I didn't used to think he talked much. He does. Or can. I didn't know he was interested in space. He is. I didn't know he could get excited about things. He can. But nothing gives him goosebumps. Not even infinity. Which reminds him of *water*.

Oh yeah — and he carries a wallet. With a picture of his grandmother in it.

Well, if I couldn't get him to break out in goosebumps, at least I could find out a little more about the grandmother business. It turns out that his grandmother didn't want to leave Korea with the rest of her family. This was when Peter's parents were just little. So she stayed behind. When Peter was born she wrote and said her only rgeret in staying over there was not being able to see him. Then she got real sick, when Peter was still a baby, but before she died, she got these envelopes and inside each one she put a little dried flower. Then she sealed the envelopes up and wrote a different year on each one. Then she sent them to Peter and died.

So now there's a stack of envelopes in Peter's room, and every year he opens one up.

I asked him where he puts the flowers.

"In a box," he said.

"Like a special box?"

He shook his head yes.

"How many envelopes did she send you, Peter?" I asked him.

"A hundred," he said.

I couldn't get Peter Kim and his grandmother out of my head. I felt guilty. There I was with six grandparents: two from my mother, two from my father, and two from Ham. (I count them in because I know how much old people love to have grandkids—and Ham's their only kid. Besides, imagine saying "stepgrandmother.") But Peter—all he had was a picture. Not even a memory.

Then I got an idea. I thought about it and I worked on it and I made it. I called it the Freeze-Dried Grandmother Launch Pad.

It all has to do with this stuff I read about and asked my science teacher and Ham about. Speed and space and time aren't just separate things. They have something to do with each other. For instance, the faster *you* go, the slower *time* goes. Which means, if you can go really fast, like around the speed of light (which we can't actually; not yet, anyway), you can get older slower. In other words, you can stay young a long time. But here's the *really* mind-blowing part: if you can go *faster* than the speed of light, you might even start going backward in time. You could get younger and younger —till you're a baby again!

So here's what they do. First, as soon as a grandmother dies, they freeze-dry her. Sort of like coffee. Then they just wait around till there's a grandkid born. Okay. They launch him off. But not *too* fast. They don't want him to stop growing, or even slow down much. The idea is to get him out there real far. Say out around Alpha Centauri, the nearest star. He just goes into orbit around it. Waiting. Growing.

Okay. Now. The grandmother. They put her into the Freeze-Dried Grandmother Launch Pad and send her off. Now this one is *really* fast. Out it goes, faster and faster, and pretty soon that grandmother is going as fast as light. Then *faster* than light. She's the fastest thing in the whole universe. And so her time is different from everything else's time. Her time starts to go backward. It goes back to the day she died. And then she un-dies, and it's the day before she died, and then a week before, and she's going faster and faster and getting younger and younger, and by the time she reaches Alpha Centauri she's only about fifty years old. Or maybe even forty.

And there waiting for her is her grandchild. The one who was born after she died. Now's the tricky part, because what she has to do is slow down. And that means she'll start getting old again and die. She locates her grandson's ship and throttles down and slips into his orbit, and pretty soon their ships are side by side. They go to the portals and look out at each other and talk to each other by shortwave and laugh and say anything they want. But mostly they just look. She's getting old again real fast now, and there's only time for one trip around the star. But it's better than nothing. It's better than just a picture in a wallet.

When I got the Freeze-Dried Grandmother Launch Pad finished, I took it to school and told Peter to come over to my locker and gave it to him. I told him it was to help him get his own space station started. I told him how it worked.

He just kept looking down at it. He didn't say anything, but his arm was full of goosebumps.

SNOW

Snow! First of the year.

It started in the morning during math class. Not everybody agreed at first. Some people said it was snow. Others said it was just ashes from a fire. It *was* hard to tell.

But by the end of class the arguments were over. It was snow, all right.

By the end of English it was heavy; big fat globs coming down.

Nobody could eat at lunch. In the kitchen you could see them scraping tons of food into the garbage cans. The middle of the lunchroom was empty except for the monitors. Everybody else was hanging around the windows.

Walking through the long hallways, where there were only lockers and walls and ceilings, everybody would kind of get nervous and hurry till they came to a window.

By the first class of the afternoon it was piling up on the windowsills. Things got quieter and quieter. Ralphie Smitht laughed out loud in the morning, but from noontime on he only grinned. The teachers' voices seemed far away. They were asking questions, but there weren't any answers. The snow piled higher and higher on the sills. It splattered against the windowpanes, like soft, silent explosions. It was piling up all around — you could *feel* it — on the main doorsteps, at the boys and girls gym doors in the back, on the bike racks, on the bushes. It was on the roof. Getting deeper. Deeper. A great soft, silent pillow. Pressing. Hugging.

It wanted us to come out.

Oh, they tried. They tried to keep us there forever. But they couldn't stop the clock, and when the last bell rang we were gone. G-O-N-E. The teachers flattened themselves against the walls. In three seconds flat that school was empty. E-M-P-T-Y.

And no one told us, and no one told them, but we knew, and they knew we knew: no school the next day.

We didn't take the bus home. We walked. And planned.

We figured we wouldn't do anything real special that night. Just sort of cruise and throw snowballs and push each other and do general snow stuff. The only definite thing would be going over to Calvin's house for hot chocolate.

Then the next day. A whole day. First we decided we'd go sledding. We have our own private place to go. It's a golf course. You just go over the fence and past these evergreen trees and this little lake and there it is: the perfectest sledding hill you ever saw. Nobody else knows about it. And all of us — me, Richie, Peter, Calvin, and Dugan — we all swore to God (Dugan crossed himself) never to tell anybody.

As for the sleds, Calvin is the only one that has a real one. The kind that's wood, with runners. The rest of us have those round aluminum giant dishes that you hold on to with hand-straps and sail down the hill on your butt on. Which is what we do — racing. And when we get tired of that, we all climb onto Calvin's sled, all *five* of us, stacked on top of each other, and down the hill. It's terrifying being on top — four bodies weaving under you — but it's the funnest part too.

And then Dugan said let's make a snow hut. By the time he got done saying how neat it would be inside — you could build a little fire and eat and it would even be warm — we all wanted to do that too.

So we decided to do both. Sled *and* snow hut.

We were walking and messing around and planning so long that it was dinner time when I got home. I was pretty excited. I couldn't relax. I wanted to get out and meet the guys as soon as I could. I must have been eating pretty fast, because I remember hearing Ham say, "My God, honey, look how *alive* he is. He's not even taking the time to *swallow!*"

Where did it get me? Instead of heading out to meet the guys, next thing I know I'm out on the sidewalk — shoveling. I gave Ham a million reasons why I shouldn't have to do it, not right then anyway. But he didn't care. Grownups with kids of shovel-age know they have a good thing:

1. They don't have to do it themselves.
2. They can make the kid do it.
3. They don't have to pay.

When I asked him what about Mary, he said she was the one that did the driveway. "Mary had it done by the time I got home," he said. (Vomit.)

And what about him? "Oh, I think I'll just stay in here where it's nice and warm," he goes, smirking. "Since I never do any work anyway, as you're always telling me, it wouldn't be right for me to start now, now would it? Maybe I'll just put on my robe and slippers and read a book; or smoke that ol' pipe; or curl up —" That's the last I heard before I slammed the door shut.

Well, I'll tell you one thing: it didn't take me all night to shovel that sidewalk.

Turned out everybody else had to shovel too. Except Dugan, of course. When we finally got together we headed in the general direction of the Monroe School. It's hard to explain. I mean, nobody said, "Let's go to Monroe." We just headed that way. Like animals heading for the waterhole. All over that part of town, packs of kids were out prowling, and most of them, sooner or later, would wind up at Monroe. Then there'd be a herd.

On the way we threw snowballs at two things: each other and cars. I tried not to throw too many at cars, and I only aimed at their backs. I know you're not supposed to throw at cars. But just go ahead and be a kid and try not to. Just try. And besides, it's not fair. If they're not going to let you drive cars, the least they can do is let you throw snowballs at them.

We joined the herd at Monroe. Just sort of walked around at first. Seeing what was what. It was pretty dark. You could just about make out the shapes of kids. Mostly it was voices. Screams. You listened for ones you recognized. (I knew Debbie Breen's regular voice, but I wasn't sure about her scream.) And names.

The more you looked and listened, the more you saw there were kids everywhere. The big front steps. The driveway. The bushes. The playground. You'd hear the swings creaking before you could see anybody on them. You'd pass under the sliding board — look up — somebody would be on top. Monkey bars too.

Everybody was either in a tight little group, planning, or

they were having a snowball fight, or they were chasing each other. No lone wolves. And unless you were close, it was almost impossible to tell boys from girls — by looking anyway. The best way to do it was to single out one of the dark figures, say, one running in the open, and wait till it screamed. Then you'd know what it was.

Once around the school we went, and nothing happened. So Dugan packed a good snowball, snuck up right behind somebody standing still, took about five minutes aiming — we were cracking up — and let the kid have it. The fight was on!

It was a great fight. It kind of flowed around the school. Pretty soon everyone was in on it, and it was everywhere. We were firing from the steps, firing from the trees, firing from the bushes. There were little skirmishes on the sides. There were snipers in the monkey bars. There were massacres in the corners and stepwells. There were banzai attacks. People retreated to the sidewalks, into the gutters, then they counterattacked and beat the others back to the school.

It was actually a pretty organized war. But to the grownups passing by it probably just looked like a mess of snowballs and moosecalls.

There was something else too, which I found out when I was looking for a hiding place for a minute. There were The Lovers, making out in a bush.

All the time I kept my ears peeled for Debbie Breen. I was pretty sure she was there. I bumped into one of her girlfriends. I thought I heard her name called out a couple times. I even thought I heard her herself. But whenever I went to where I thought she was, she wasn't.

I wondered if the other Skywalker was there. I still didn't find out who he was. I made it a point to pelt anybody tall I saw. Just in case.

Another goal was to pelt Ralphie Smitht. When snow's on the ground, that *t* on the end stands for *Target*. You know how it's impossible not to kick a can when it's right there in the middle of the sidewalk in front of you? Well, it's just as impossible not to pelt Ralphie Smitht. And of course, the more you hit him, the more he laughs. He *enjoys* it.

But hitting Ralphie isn't all that much fun after the first couple throws. There's no satisfaction. He's too easy. Besides, your throwing arm could fall off before you'd make him stop laughing. So what you do is, you just sort of pelt him as a sideline, when there isn't anything better to do at the moment.

That's what I was doing when I saw what every good snowballer is always looking for: a moving target out in the open. It was alone. It was running. It was outlined against the streetlights.

I didn't think. I acted. I packed hard the ball I already had in my hand for Ralphie, wheeled, rushed up to get closer, set myself good in the snow, wound up, aimed, fired. All this only took about one and a half seconds.

I hit the target. Dead center in the side of the head. (Something flashed through my brain: *Jesus! People ain't like birds. You can hit them.*) It screamed. It fell. It was a girl. It was Debbie Breen.

I turned around and started firing like crazy at Ralphie Smitht. The more Debbie screamed the harder I threw, and the harder I threw the more Ralphie laughed. It seemed like

I was scooping and throwing for hours. Finally I went right up to him, like an executioner. He just stood there, sort of grinning and wincing with his hands flapped over his head, and that's where I fired the last one, point-blank.

I kept on walking. I forced myself not to run. Behind me Debbie was screaming bloody murder. Some of her girlfriends came running past me, yelling her name. Then almost everybody was rushing.

I sort of wandered around the building out to the front. It was deserted, except for The Lovers. They even came out of their bush to listen. You could still hear the screaming plain on the other side of the school.

I wanted to keep on walking home, but I was afraid that would give me away. So I just hung around the sidewalk and lobbed some balls at a tree. I wondered if anybody saw me. I kept half expecting a voice out of the night: "Herkimer! He did it! There he is! Let's get him!" And then the mob.

I knew she didn't see me. But did anybody else? Maybe they did. But maybe, in the dark, they didn't know who it was. Ralphie Smitht — he must have. But for some reason I didn't think he would tell.

The screaming stopped. *God!* I thought. *Maybe she's dead. I killed her. Jesus, please, no! Of all people! NO!*

Cold, wet, icy snow smashed me in the face. Snow gorged up my nose. Into my mouth. Snow pressed against my eyeballs. My lids couldn't come down. My eyeballs felt like ice marbles.

Somebody was mashing a whole armload of snow into my face. I groped out for his hands and arms, but he was pretty strong and kept mashing. I could hear him grunting. I couldn't see. I could hardly breathe.

Finally I got hold of an arm and yanked around and we both wound up on the ground, in the snow, me on the bottom, facedown, these hands pressing my face into the snow. And all of a sudden I realized what was going on. Somebody *did* see me. Whoever it was didn't tell anybody, because there was no mob. He was just taking care of me himself. Probably the other Luke Skywalker. I didn't care. I was getting what I deserved. Let him do whatever he wanted. I had it coming. I stopped fighting back.

As soon as I stopped, he stopped. The hands were off my head.

I wiped my face. Scooped snow out of my neck. I stayed on the ground. I wasn't too anxious to look. After a while I sort of creaked my head around. He was there okay, standing right over me. I saw boots, pants, a fur-trimmed jacket, a face — the *wrong* face. It wasn't a him. It was a her. It was the trombone girl. McAllister.

She was staring straight down at me. At first she looked kind of funny. Probably wondering why I stopped fighting back. Then she smiled, if you want to call it that, and she said, "Now we're even." Then she walked off, slow, past the school, down the street.

I was just getting up when I heard a crowd coming. *They're after me too!* I'm thinking. But they weren't. They were taking Debbie home.

She was walking in the middle of them. Her hat was off. She was holding her ear with both hands and sobbing. I couldn't see any blood, but it was really sad. I prayed I didn't break her eardrum. She went right by me, and under the streetlight you could see her whole face was red and shining with tears, and her mouth was blue and all stretched out of shape from crying. Her watery eyes landed on me for a second, but they didn't seem to see. When she was past, something seemed to reach out of my chest and go clawing after her, pleading, "I'm sorry, Debbie . . . really really sorry. Please forgive me. . . ."

The rest of the snow time, that night and the next day, I just sort of went through the motions. I went along with the other guys to Calvin's for hot chocolate. But I didn't really taste it, and the steam coming up from the mug was like guilt in my face.

We went to the golf course and did our sledding. I didn't push too hard on the aluminum butt-bouncer. I just let the hill take me. When we piled onto Calvin's sled, I didn't fight the other guys for the top. I just stayed in the middle.

Kippy Kim was there. Peter had to bring him, as usual. About the only fun I had was watching him throw tantrums because we always took off down the hill before he could climb onto the pile.

As for the snow hut, I didn't mind building it, but it didn't do too much for me just to sit inside it. We made a little fire, but that didn't work too good because we forgot to put in a chimney. Richie brought some pancake syrup from home, and some paper cups, and we filled them with clean snow and poured the syrup on.

That night when I got home I called up one of Debbie's girlfriends and told her I heard Debbie got hurt and asked how she was. She was okay, she said. No problems. No broken eardrum. Probably be in school the next day.

I was really glad to hear all that. But even after I hung up I still didn't feel right.

WAITING

NOTHING MUCH HAPPENED THEN FOR A WHILE. IT NEVER DOES. Not at that time of year, with Christmas just a couple weeks away. If time goes faster at the speed of light, well, around now it's riding on the back of a snail. An *old* snail.

In December there are two main things you do:

1. You wait.
2. You work on your Christmas list.

We're always supposed to have our lists in by December 1. But how can you do that? That leaves twenty-four days to look in stores. Twenty-four days to see what other people have that you could use. Twenty-four days of TV commercials. Twenty-four days to change your mind. You can't do it. So I always come up later with a revised version. And then a final revised version. And then an absolutely final revised version (with last-minute changes). I know I have to stop when Ham smiles, takes the list, nods, goes "Mm-hmm. Mm-hmm," and then, still smiling, very, very neat and slow, tears the paper until it's almost confetti, and drops the pieces back in my hand.

What bugs me more than anything else about a Christmas list is having to listen to somebody make comments on it. They can't just take the thing and then just get or not get you the stuff. Oh no. It has to be, "Hey, whoa, hold it there. *What* is *this*?"

Or, "Didn't we just get you one of these last year?"

Or, "Were you thinking of paying for half of this yourself?"

Naturally most of this kind of talk comes from Ham. That's what I hate about him sometimes: he always has to *say* something about something. My mother's not like that. She understands kids better. She's more reasonable. That's why I always try to give my list to her.

But she always lets Ham see it. ("Honey," she says to me, "Ham *has* to see it. He's the one that pays for all this, you know.")

I hate it the most when he doesn't say anything, but just starts laughing.

This year Ham's big comment is, "What, no dinosaurs?" Each time I hand in an updated list I hear it. I even hear it other times too, like when I'm going to bed, or going to the bathroom. Anywhere. Anytime. Like a cuckoo. "What, no dinosaurs? What, no dinosaurs?"

This year I hadn't asked to get dinosaurs, but I was going to give them. That's what I decided to get Timmy for Christmas. Just a couple cheap ones. Like the ones everybody knows: brontosaurus and *Tyrannosaurus rex*. I figure if I get him some of his own, maybe he'll stop taking mine.

Except for anything that Cootyhead does, including breathing, there's not many things that I hate more than

Timmy taking my dinosaurs. It's not that I can't stand to share anything with him. It's just that my dinosaurs aren't toys. They're a collection. They're not to play with. They're really good ones. They cost a lot. It took me a long time to get hold of them. I don't have just the famous ones, like the ones I mentioned, and triceratops and stegosaurus. I have other ones. Ones you probably never heard of. Ones you never saw in a Japanese movie. Plateosaurus. Ornithomimus. Trachodon.

I had to move them from my room when my space station started getting too big, so I put them on a platform in the basement. I got cardboard and twigs and a papier-mâché volcano and stuff and made it look like sixty million years ago. And then I put the dinosaurs in. And in front of each one I made a little sign telling what it is.

All that — and nobody understands why I get all mad when I see one of them is missing and I go looking around and finally find it lying in the dirt outside. Or in the bathtub.

So Timmy goes bawling, if he's playing with it when I find it and jerk it from him, and my mother goes, "Well, he didn't hurt it, did he?"

"I don't care," I tell her. "That's beside the point."

"He was only playing with it."

"It's not to play with. It's not a toy."

"Well, it looks like a toy to him. Don't you think?"

"It's *not*. It's my col-*lec*-tion!"

"I know, I know," she nods and looks at Timmy. "Now, Timmy, you know these are Jason's collection. They're not toys. You do not take them out of the basement —"

"Off the platform —" I go.

"Off the platform —"

"Don't touch them —"

"Don't touch them —"

"Ever."

"Ever. Never never never touch them — not even with the tippy-tip-tip of your tippy-nippy nose. Understand?"

So my mother's there tweaking Timmy's nose and he's there laughing and everybody's having a great old time except me, who's standing there fuming with a dirty dinosaur in my hand. As you can see, my mother is really rough. She'd make a great Marine drill sergeant.

So naturally, he keeps taking my dinosaurs.

When I told my mother what I was getting Timmy for Christmas, she goes, "Jason, why don't you just let him have yours. You don't play with them anymore."

She still didn't understand. "I know I don't play with them," I said. "You're not supposed to. They're a collection. You're supposed to *look* at them."

"You're supposed to add to them too, aren't you?"

"I almost have them all," I told her. "I can't find any more."

"I never see you looking at them."

"I can't help that. I *do* look."

"Don't get smart."

"I do."

"You took them out of your room."

"Yeah — to make room for the space station. You're the one that said it was a flophouse up there."

"Flophouse? Did I say that?"

"Forget it," I said. I walked away.

She calls. "Jason."

"What?"

"You got them in the toy departments, didn't you?"

Screams. Fists. Atomic bombs.

So, to get Ham to stop saying "What, no dinosaurs?" and to show my mother I was still interested in them, I grabbed my Christmas list back and added to it in giant red letters:

PODOKESAURUS

When people think of dinosaurs they think of the biggest animals that ever roamed the earth. But that's not the whole truth. Dinosaurs came in all sizes. There were medium-size ones. And little ones too. The littlest dinosaur was podokesaurus. It wasn't much bigger than a chicken. Imagine little dinosaurs running around a barnyard. Or seeing them all lined up under plastic wrap on the meat counter at the A&P. Imagine.

Like I said, I just did it to get Ham and Mom off my back. I know they won't be able to find a podokesaurus. I never could. But that doesn't mean I'm giving up either. Podokesaurus is still the only one missing from my collection — or at least the only one I really care about — and even though when I grow up I might lose some of my interest, no matter where I am or what I'm doing, I'll always keep an eye out for the chicken-size dinosaur.

Well, I won. Sort of. Ham knocked off the dinosaur stuff, all right. He started in with a new one: "Aha: clothes!"

On the last Saturday night before Christmas we had to go to a play. One that Ham was in. Except for Timmy — he got a babysitter. I told my mother I'd be glad to babysit, but she dragged me and Cootyhead along.

It was in an old barn. At least it used to be a barn. They took out the hay and the cowpoop and put in these crummy old benches and this dinky stage without even a curtain. And that's supposed to be a theater. I always thought Ham acted in a *real* theater. Velvet curtain. Strings of lightbulbs. Posters. Uh-uh. It's a barn.

The play was too long. It was about this salesman. That was Ham. I never figured out what he was supposed to be selling. His name was Willy.

Ham's voice sounded funny. It was lower. And they made his hair gray. He had a wife and two sons. They were pretty much grown up, but they were still living at home. One of them was named Biff, I think. He kept talking about going out west and having a ranch.

The whole thing didn't make any sense. I mean, nothing happened. Biff talked about going out west, and Willy was going off selling something, and then he lost his job and then he begged his boss to give it back but he wouldn't, and every once in a while this old dude in a suit pops out and goes, "Ah went intuh the jungle, and when Ah came out — bah God — Ah was rich!"

Another weird thing: people didn't come onto the stage from the sides or behind. I mean, there wasn't any backstage. They just stood at the end of the aisle between the benches where the audience (us) came in, and ran down the aisle and onto the stage from the front. Like I said, it wasn't a real theater.

So I happen to be sitting on the end of our bench, next to the aisle, and we're toward the back, and this one time I look over and up and who's standing right next to me but Ham. About an inch away. He looked even goofier close up. They even made his eyebrows gray. His cheeks were orange.

I kept waiting for him to look down and give me one of his weird looks or clever comments. But he didn't. He just stared straight ahead at the stage. His head was nodding a little and his Adam's apple was going and his lips were moving. I knew he knew I was right there. The more he didn't look at me the more I was tempted to tap him on the leg. I don't know why. It just sort of made me mad, him acting like I wasn't there. I was going to give him a shot in the knee and tell him, "Hey — who you trying to fool? You're Ham." Just then his whole face changes. He roars something from right over my head, tears down the aisle, and next thing you know there he is up on stage, in the spotlight.

At long last the end came. I was just about asleep by then. I only remember someone going, "We're free. . . . We're free. . . ." I was surprised at how loud the clapping got when they took their bows. Ham got the loudest.

When we were walking out I asked my mother, "What happened to Ham?"

"You mean Willy?"

"Yeah."

"Weren't you watching?"

"Yeah."

"Well," she said, "Willy dies."

On the last day of school before Christmas I went to a basketball game. Not to see the game — we're crummy in basketball — but to see Debbie Breen. She was cheerleading.

For a couple days after the snowball fight at Monroe, she was in school with a patch on her ear. It was really cute, because the patch stopped about halfway down her earlobe, so she could put her earring on.

One day I finally got up the nerve, and I said to her, "Hey, we got something in common."

"What's that?" she goes. It was the first time I looked her

in the eye since I hit her. I could tell she never knew it was me.

I said, "We both had patches. Me on my eye, you on your ear."

"Hey," she goes, "that's right!"

I was so surprised and happy by the way she acted — all excited and friendly — that all of a sudden I wanted to say all kinds of stuff. Stuff that was boiling inside me for days: It was me that hit you with the snowball and I hope you'll forgive me now. I'd chop off my little finger to stop you from crying. Are you ready to come see my space station now? How about tonight? I think about you all the time. Do you ever think about me? You're beautiful. Wanna go for a pizza? I wish I could give you a Christmas present. I'd get you anything you want. Do you like me? I love you. Do you think we could ever get married someday? Who were you with on Halloween?

But I didn't say any of that. I said, "Go on any hayrides lately?"

And she said, "Kill any dragons lately?"

We laughed. It was like marshmallows melting together.

During the basketball game I watched every move she made. On the court cheering. On the bench. I liked seeing all that bare leg. During the winter about all you ever see is face. I imagined what she'd look like cheering in high school. Splits. Cartwheels. Handstands. Tights. She flicked her head a lot.

A couple girls were sitting behind me. I heard one of them say, "Who's that one?"

And the other one said, "Debbie somebody."

And the first one said, "She's pretty."

I smiled to myself: *Yeah, she's pretty all right. That's Debbie Breen. I went on a hayride with her. That's right — that cheerleader. I roasted her hotdogs and marshmallows. We talk to each other. Yeah. She kinda likes me. She's coming over to my house to see my space station. We'll probably start going together pretty soon.*

They did a cheer where each of the cheerleaders had one of the letters of our nickname: Bulldogs. Like the first one would jump up and yell: "Gimme a B!" and everybody in the stands yells: "B!"

Debbie had the second L. At least to everybody else she did. Not to me. I sort of sat back for the rest of the game, with my eyes half closed, and here's what I saw in the middle of the court: Debbie Breen, hanging in the air, legs wide, arms to the lights, sweater bottom halfway up her stomach, screaming at the stands — at the world — with all her heart:

"GIMME A J!"

On the last day before Christmas I got sick. I threw up. I ached all over. I couldn't move. I couldn't believe it. Sick. Of all times! My mother kept bringing me tea and asking if I wanted soup and softboiled eggs. I couldn't get out of bed. I was dying. *God, no. Let me die* after *Christmas!*

The head of my bed is next to the window overlooking the yard. Every once in a while I dragged my head up enough to look out. There was snow on the ground. Once I saw a squirrel go by. I kept looking, and in a minute he came back the other way. I kept looking and the squirrel kept doing it, back and forth, back and forth. Dug his own little trench in the snow. I could only see that corner of the yard, so I couldn't tell where he was going or where he was coming from. I could only see him racing, and that's what he was doing: racing. Like something was after him. I got tired and lay back down. When I looked again, later, there he was, back and forth, back and forth — racing, racing . . .

And then I got the weirdest, craziest feeling: *the squirrel was trying to make me better.* I didn't know why, or how. I couldn't see where he was coming from or going to. But there he was — back and forth, back and forth, racing, all day long — and I just couldn't get that crazy idea out of my head.

And sure enough, next day, Christmas, I was better.

PRESENTS

MY PILE WAS IN THE MIDDLE, SIZE-WISE. BIGGER THAN MOM'S and Ham's. Smaller than Timmy's and Cootyhead's. I didn't care. I had a *quality* pile. For instance, I got a digital watch. It hardly took up any room, but I wouldn't trade it for Cootyhead's twirling baton or Timmy's giant clown balloon.

The other good things I got were a pocket calculator, three rolls of aluminum foil for my space station, and a bunch of clothes. No podokesaurus, of course.

When Timmy opened up the dinosaurs, I could tell right away he didn't like them as much as mine. He was craziest about his Tommy gun. He calls it a Thomas gun.

My mother liked the notepaper I got her. With matching envelopes with a design on the inside.

Ham liked his book. *Burbage: Greatest Shakespearean Actor.*

One good thing about a broken family: when you open your last Christmas present at home, and you're sad because there aren't any more, all of a sudden it occurs to you you

123

still have one parent to go. There's another Christmas coming up.

We went to my father's the next day, me and Cootyhead. Timmy was all upset because he couldn't come. He wanted two fathers too, so he could get a double dose of presents. I told him my father got him a big pile of presents anyway, but since he wasn't coming along I was going to have to keep them for myself. As usual he started bawling, and as usual I had to tell him I was only kidding.

My mother gets furious with me for teasing him, but she can't stop me. *I* can't stop me. I take one look at him and out it comes. Like, "There's a tarantula over your head." Or, "They're coming to wreck our house today." Or, "*We're* having Sloppy Joes for dinner. *You're* having flies."

Actually it's Timmy's fault. If he didn't believe everything I say, maybe I'd stop.

Ham drove me and Cootyhead to the station. From there we took the train into the city. I sat at the window on one side of the aisle, she sat on the other.

Coming into the city, you'd never know it was Christmas from the looks of the ratty backyards of some black neighborhoods we passed. I was glad Calvin didn't live there. I wondered if they had candles or wreaths or anything in the front.

When we got off the train and met my father, a lady was with him. My father looked happy and a little proud. He said her name so loud and slow and clear, like an announcement, that I kind of glanced around to see who else he was talking to.

"Children," he said, "may I present to you — Miss . . . Barbara . . . Silverstein."

She looked okay. She wasn't the first girlfriend we ever saw my father with. But it was the first time we ever saw one outside his apartment. And the first time we ever got a last name. She had perfume on.

"Is she Jewish?" I whispered to my father on the way to his place.

He winked. He never winked before in his life. "Is the Pope Catholic?" he goes.

That's when I started worrying about the presents. I remembered Jews don't have Christmas, and the holiday they do have is the one where you just get one present a day for eight days. I wondered if the Jews let him join since we saw him last. And even if they didn't, maybe he was trying to impress Barbara Silverstein. Maybe if he had Christmas stuff in his apartment, she wouldn't like him. Maybe she was a plant. Maybe she was only tricking my father into thinking she liked him, when all the time she was really sent over by some rabbi to check out to see if he qualified. Maybe that's what my father was trying to tell me with the wink, I had to be careful.

Dad was driving, with Barbara Silverstein riding shotgun. She kept turning around to talk to us in the back. She was clever, all right, trying to see how Gentile we were.

Like she said, "Well, did you kids have a merry Christmas?"

"Merry what?" I said. But she didn't notice, because Cootyhead was already telling her all the stuff she got. Cootyhead instantly adores every one of my dad's girlfriends. She wants him to get married again.

"Hanukkah wasn't bad either," I said.

I could tell by her expression, that took her by surprise.

But she recovered quick. "And how about you, Jason? Did you get a lot of presents too?"

"Oh . . . one," I said.

"Gee," she goes, "is that all?"

"Mm . . . not really," I said. I looked her straight in the eye. "I got seven more coming."

Cootyhead squeals, "Waddaya mean? You got lotsa stuff!"

As soon as Barbara Silverstein turned, I kicked my stupid sister. "Dad-deee!" she bawls. "He's kicking me!" She picks up the windshield ice scraper and hits me about fifty times with it.

But my mind's on other things. "Hey Dad," I said. "Have any lox lately?"

I could see her ears perk up.

"You bet," he said. "I'd be eating it if it was *twenty* dollars a pound."

Great answer, Dad, I thought. *Now we're cooking.*

"Bagels too?" I said.

"By the bushel," he said.

"Find any new delis lately?" I said.

"None left to find," he said. "I have been to every deli within a twenty-five-mile radius." Barbara Silverstein laughed. My father looked at her. "It's true," he said.

Hear that, Barbara Silverstein?

I kept trying to think of all I knew about Jews from Marty Renberg. I asked my father if he had a good time at church —on *Saturday*. And if he stomped on any glasses at a wedding lately. And if he was being careful not to mess around with any ham.

His answers didn't always make too much sense. Not to me anyway. I could see Barbara Silverstein taking notes in her head. In fact I was sure she had a little recorder in her pocketbook.

As it turned out, we didn't go right back to my father's place. We went to see the Ice Capades. It was part of our present. Barbara Silverstein and my father sat in the middle, between me and Cootyhead. Except when they were clapping, they held hands the whole time.

Every once in a while, when the show got a little boring (I would've rather gone to a football or basketball game), I would ask Barbara Silverstein something. Like, "Did you ever go to Israel?" And, "Do rabbis get married?" And, "Do you know Marty Renberg?"

About halfway through the show she got up and left (either for the bathroom or to check in with her boss rabbi). She left her pocketbook under her seat. I saw my chance. I reached down for it.

"I better hold this till she comes back," I said to my father. He nodded. "Good idea."

Then, when he was busy watching, I sort of slouched myself so my mouth was near the pocketbook. I couldn't risk opening it. I could only hope the hidden recorder would hear me. I waited for the next applause. And soon as it came, I whisper-said into the pocketbook, "Bill Herkimer? Ah yes, he's the Jewish fellow, isn't he? No? Goodness, he certainly fooled me." I made my voice sound different, like a man-in-the-street interview.

When the next applause came I changed my voice again and said, "Bill Herkimer. . . . Sure! The one with all the Jewish friends."

Next time: "Herkimer . . . Herkimer . . . You must mean the fellow that has that great supply of beanies."

Then: "Bill Herkimer . . . y'know, I always said that guy'd make a great Jew."

Then Barbara Silverstein came back.

Well, I did all I could. I just settled back and watched the rest of the show. When we got back to my father's, things got a little confusing again. The presents *were* there. Two Gentile type all-in-one-day piles. Along with a little silver tree on the coffee table and a big red and white Styrofoam candy cane on the apartment door. I mean, any way you looked at it it spelled C-H-R-I-S-T-M-A-S.

And Barbara Silverstein was right there, soaking it all in. The only thing I could think was, my father figured he owed us a Christmas, and he was going to see that we got one. Even if it cost him points with the Jews.

Late that night, after Barbara Silverstein left, Cootyhead asks her usual question: "You gonna marry her, Daddy?"

My father took off his shoes. It hit me that for the first time since he moved away, his shoes weren't white. He was changing. "Probably," he said. What he didn't do was the usual stuff, like lift Cootyhead up to the ceiling or tickle her and say cutesy things like, "Now what would you do if I said yes?" No. He didn't even look up. He just kept pulling his shoes off and kind of nodded a little and said "Probably" about marrying Barbara Silverstein. Like he would say "baked" if a waitress asked him how he wanted his potato.

That's how I knew — not from what he said, but how, and his shoes weren't white — that Barbara Silverstein was going to be my stepmother.

When I got him alone the next day I asked him if he wasn't still trying to join the Jews.

"Letting that slide for a while, J.T.," he says. He calls me

J.T. sometimes when we're one-on-one. My middle name is Theodore. (Ugh!)

"Why?" I asked him.

"Why?" he goes. He breathed long. "Oh, I don't know. Hard to say."

I was disappointed. Some of the best times I had with my father were when he took us around to delis and told us all about Jewish stuff. I was even thinking of trying to become one myself. "Remember how you said the Jew knows how to live?" I asked him.

He grinned. "Yeah, I remember. I'm not saying that's not true."

"You still go to delis?"

"Yep, right. Still go to delis. But y'see, that's . . . that's . . . not it. That's not . . . being Jewish."

"So what is?" I asked him.

He lit up one of those straight little cigars with the plastic tip. That was new too. He used to smoke cigarettes.

"Well," he said, "I'm not even sure. I just know what it's not. And it's not delis and cream sodas and Miami Beach."

"Or lox and bagels?"

"Or lox and bagels."

"Or stomping on glasses?"

"Or stomping on glasses."

"Or wearing beanies?"

He blew out a thin stream of smoke and gave me a winking smile. "It's all rigamarole," he said.

"What's rigamarole?"

He tapped ashes. The cigar end went from gray to orange. "Well, it's like what we were just saying. It's doing all these fancy—uh—maneuverings. Without really knowing why you're doing them."

I said, "Do just the Jews have rigamarole?"

He chuckled. "Everybody has rigamarole, J.T. Lotta action. Lotta noise."

"Protestants and Catholics?"

"Sure. Everybody." He pointed the cigar at me. "That doesn't make a religion bad, understand. That doesn't mean it's not good or it's not real. It's just that the real stuff is down at the bottom, and you have to dig to get at it."

"Like clams."

"That's it: like clams. See, Barbara — she took me to a synagogue once, and she gave me some books to read, and, uh, well, I'll tell you what she said." He snuffed out the cigar and took out another one, but he didn't light it. "She said, 'Look, if you want to convert to Judaism, fine. But don't do it to play a game or because I'm a Jew. Do it because you feel the need to do it deep inside. Because you *have* to. Because your soul won't rest until it's done. Don't convert unless you're going to become the best Jew you can possibly be. Otherwise you're just playing games. And anyway, I love you the way you are.' " My father lit up, cleared his throat. "That's what she said. Can't argue with that, huh?"

"Guess not," I said.

All that didn't mean a whole lot to me, except that now I don't know what to believe and what not to believe about Jews. The thing about grownups is, they go changing things on you, only they don't tell you about it till afterward. It might be a rug they changed, or a lampshade or a parent. Either way, just when you think you're sure about things — poof — they're different.

I said, "I guess you don't like the present I got you too much then, huh?" What I got him was this book called *The Rabbi Never Knocks Twice*.

"Hey," he goes. He's scowling at me.

"What?"

"Did I say I liked it?"

"Yeah."

"Okay then." His eyes were examining me. He sort of wandered over and held his hand out. "Gimme five," he said.

I gave him five.

"And you still like lox and bagels?" I said.

"Hey," he goes, "does a fish know how to swim?"

When my father put me and Cootyhead on the train, it was only three o'clock in the afternoon. We didn't get home till almost nine. The trip usually takes forty-five minutes.

Here's what happened:

The train broke down. They brought a bus to get us. We got mixed up and got off the bus at the wrong stop. We used the last of our money to buy two tickets to Avon Oaks. We kept listening for the conductor to say "A-a-a-vonoaks." He never did. We must have made another mistake. We wound up back in the city.

"We're gonna get killed," Cootyhead kept saying. She meant killed by Ham and my mom. I wasn't worried about them. I was worried about getting killed by muggers.

We bummed a dime from a lady to make a phone call. (Actually Cootyhead bummed it. She'll ask anybody for anything. No shame.) We argued about who to call. We called my father. No answer. Called home. No answer.

"They're waiting for us at the station," I said.

"We're gonna get killed," she said.

My sister wanted to ask somebody for train fare home. That's where I drew the line. I'd rather take my chances with the muggers than ask a stranger for a couple dollars. I figured the best thing was to go back to my father's. He probably just stepped out to a deli for a minute anyway. And even if he wasn't there, we could use a neighbor's phone.

I walked out of the station. Cootyhead had to follow.

I let her ask people for directions. I knew we were only about seven or eight minutes away by car. That couldn't be too far.

We started walking. It was bad enough that we had to walk the city streets. It was twice as bad because of what we were carrying: presents. We each had our presents in a pillowcase. (Except for my prize present: a solid-state LCD microprocessor pocket-size football game. I kept that in my pocket.) We do it that way every year. The grownups on the train on the way home always think we're adorable. They ask us cutesy questions. The pillowcases were white.

So there we are, walking in the city. Alone. At night. Two suburban kids. Two sackfuls of presents. White sacks. White kids. Sitting ducks.

"We're gonna get killed," she kept saying.

"Shut up!" I told her. "Just shut up!"

I kept thinking about gang wars. Kids getting shot on the corners. Crawling up the sidewalks to their front steps. Dying in their mothers' arms. They even shot them in the schoolyards!

I tried to look on the bright side:

1. Those things usually happen in the west and north and south sides of the city. We were in center city.
2. There was a girl with me. You could almost say a little girl. ("Slump down," I told her.)

I prayed for people. Crowds. Hordes. But there were only a couple of people around. And most of them were in coffee shops. We saw the backs of them on stools at the counters. And the waitresses, pouring coffee, reaching into pie shelves. Shiny urns. Meringue tops. Steam. Light. Warm. I wanted home to be a coffee shop.

We followed this street and that street, and pretty soon I had a feel for where we were. "It's right over that way," I said.

Naturally Cootyhead disagreed. She said it was another way. We argued and argued and argued. She wouldn't give in. So I started to walk. I didn't hear her follow me. I turned around. She was still there. I walked some more. Turned. Still there. More. Turned. Still there.

I hollered at her. She wouldn't budge. Then I saw the shadows move behind her. Three of them. I yelled: "Mary!"

No answer. All four figures were still. Mary was a shadow now too. All except the white sack. I called again. No one spoke. No one moved. I knew all four pairs of eyes were on me.

Except for Calvin and the others I know at school, I am afraid of black kids. Black grownups don't bother me too much. But even black girl kids and black little kids — if one of them hit me I would never hit them back. I like them, and I hate bigots and I believe black people are equal with me, but I'm still afraid of them. I think they don't like me. I think they don't even notice me in a crowd in the daytime. But on the street alone at night, I think they would know I was coming a mile away. I think sometimes about them catching me at night. I want to tell them about my friend Calvin. How I had hot chocolate at his house. How we sled stacked up down the golf course hill. But they have a knife in their hands, and they won't listen. . . .

I started to walk toward them. But not because I was brave or anything. It's just that if there's a dumb cootyhead girl that gets stopped in front of a dark alley in the city, and that girl happens to be your sister, T.S. on you. You gotta turn back. That's the way it is. Besides, I was afraid if I made them wait long they'd only get madder.

They were big kids. High school (if they didn't drop out). Trenchcoats. Wide-brim hats. Scarves. Cool. Black Dugans. Only neat.

They weren't smiling.

One of them said, "Whachoo doin' here?"

"Here?" I said. "Looking for our father's place."

Mary's eyes were as big as her white sack.

"He live here?"

"I thought so," I said.

"You don't live with him?"

"Uh, no. We live —" I caught myself. Better not tell them where.

"Where you live?" he said.

"Avon Oaks," I said.

With a long black finger he poked Mary's sack. "What's in there?"

"Uh, presents," I said. "From our father."

"You too?" he said.

I nodded. "Uh-huh."

Nobody said anything then. I took my sack from my shoulder and let it sit on the ground in front of me. *Please take them,* I thought. *You can have them all.* I was sorry I ever prayed for big piles. I was sorry I ever said "Eenie meenie mynie mo" when I was little. I was sorry I let myself laugh once when a grownup said that with the gas crisis, now they'd all have to trade in their white Cadillacs for white bicycles. *If you let us go you can have my LCD pocket football game.*

"Whu'd you get?" he said.

I shrugged. "Oh . . . stuff. Scrabble. Walkie-talkies. Clothes. You can have them."

All of a sudden one of the other two laughed. The expression on the one talking changed a little too. "You sure your father live around here?" he said.

I said I thought so.

"Where he live?" he wanted to know.

I looked at Mary. I took a deep breath. "Morville Towers," I said.

He looked shocked. "Morville Towers? That ain't around here." He jerked his head. "That's way back there." (Mary kicked me in the ankle and whispered, "Toldja.") He reached down, picked up my sack, opened it. "Presents, huh?" he goes, looking inside. Then he closed it up and slung it over his shoulder. "C'mon," he said. "We'll walk y'over there. You shouldn't be walkin' around here. Specially not at night."

They made us go ahead of them. At first nobody said much. Then the one with my sack tapped me on the shoulder. "You as scared as you look?" he said.

"Nah," I said.

He laughed. "That's it, baby. That's what I ustah say when I was goin' through white neighborhoods."

I laughed a little at that, and from then on we did more talking and laughing.

And that's how we got to be escorted all the way to my father's place.

DOUBLE DIPS

On New Year's Eve I started to get a little tired around eleven-thirty. I was already lying on the floor, so all I had to do was close my eyes. Anyway, there wasn't anything else to do but wait till midnight. I was already sick of miniature hotdogs and potato chips with onion dip and sherbet punch. (We were having our own little party.)

Sure enough, Ham noticed me. "Getting a little sleepy there, ol' boy?" he goes.

"Nah, just closin' my eyes," I told him.

"When do you want me to wake you up?" he says.

"I'm not sleeping."

"Well, just in case you accidentally doze off a little."

"I won't."

"Just in case?"

"I won't."

He leaves the room, saying, "I'll wake you at five of."

I growled, "I won't."

I did.

They say they tried to wake me. They say they even put a pan in one of my hands and a wooden spoon in the other.

But I just kept saying I knew what time it was but I didn't care, I just wanted to sleep.

Sometime during the Rose Bowl game on TV my mother asked me, "Make your New Year's resolutions yet?"

"Nah," I said. "That's a waste."

She reminded me that I used to make them.

"Yeah, I know."

"When did you stop?"

"This year."

"Oh? How's that?"

"My first resolution was to make it till midnight on New Year's Eve."

She laughed. "Maybe you shouldn't have started off with such a toughie." She sat down. For a second I thought she was interested in the game. "Y'know, I never make resolutions," she said.

I was surprised, because she always asked me about mine. "I thought you did."

"Nope," she said. "Not since I was younger than you, anyway. Then my mother showed me something better to do. At least I like it better."

"What's that?" I said.

"Well, instead of looking ahead, you look back. You look at the year you just finished. Not the one coming up."

"Why?"

"Well, I can tell you. Want to listen?"

"Yeah, okay." I was getting tired of parades and football by now anyway.

She jumped up and came back with a piece of paper and a pencil. She sat down. She looked at me. "What kind of a year do you think you had last year?" she said.

"I don't know," I said. "What do you mean?"

"I mean how would you rate last year? Great? Good? So-so? Rotten? The worst ever?"

I hate that kind of question. I was starting to regret this already. I hemmed and hawed.

"Well," she goes, "don't worry about it. Maybe I can help you out. Okay?"

I said okay.

"Now. Here's how to find out what kind of a year you had." She handed me the pencil and paper. "What I want you to do now is to write *Bad* at the top of the paper on the left . . . that's it . . . now write *Good* on the other side. Okay. Now. Very simple. You're just going to make two lists. One, of all the bad things that happened to you last year. And the other, all the good things."

"All of them?" I said.

"Well, you know what I mean. The ones you can remember. The ones worth counting."

I thought a couple seconds. The whole year was a blank. "Nothing happened," I said.

She turned off the TV. "Think," she goes. "And one thing: don't number them yet."

I thought. I started putting down some things. Like "black eye" and "suspended" and "hit friend with snowball" under *Bad*. And "hayride" and "snow day" for *Good*. The bad things really came easy: "pimple," "stolen dinosaurs," "starting seventh grade." The good ones were harder. I really had to dig for them.

"Where are you putting getting lost in the city?" my mother asked. (We told them the whole story.)

"I don't know," I said. "Was that good or bad?"

"Up to you," she said.

I put it under *Good*. I showed her the paper. The *Bad* list was a lot longer.

She looks at it. Nods. "Okay" — she hands it back — "now count them up. One point for each *Bad*, one for each *Good*."

I added them up. "Eleven to six," I told her. "Bad."

"Okay," she said. "Don't put your pencil down yet. What you have there are totals, but it's not the real score."

"Why not?"

"You didn't figure in the values. What they're worth."

I asked her what she meant.

"Well, I mean good and bad things aren't worth the same. In other words, a good apple is worth more than a bad apple. Right? A good movie is worth more than a bad movie. A good — uh, what? friend? — is worth more than a bad friend. Agree?"

I shrugged. "I guess."

"So you see," she goes, "good things are worth more than bad things. Think of it this way." She took back the paper. "This pimple here, and this hayride — you don't want to give them equal value, do you? For example, if this pimple was worth a penny, how much would you say the hayride would be worth?"

" 'Bout a thousand dollars," I said. *A million*, I thought.

She laughed. "Sure. See? So. What do we do with these lists here? Well, let's say each of the bad things is worth a one, okay?"

"Okay."

"So. We have eleven bad things. So last year was worth eleven bad points. Okay?"

"Okay."

"Now, the good things. Only six of them, right?"

"Yeah."

"But" — she raised her finger, like she was playing teacher — "as we already said, the good things are worth more. You even said a thousand times more in one case, remember?"

"Yeah."

"Well," she goes, "let's be conservative. Let's just say a good thing is only worth twice what a bad thing is worth. Okay?"

"Okay."

"And you had six good things?"

"Yeah."

"So . . ." She writes real big across the paper:

$$2 \times 6 = 12$$

She circled the 12, flaring up at the end like a piano player. "There you are. The *Good* won, twelve to eleven. You had a good year."

"News to me," I said.

"I know," she said. "A lot of people are that way. When they sit down and figure it out, it turns out they had a better year than they thought they had." She stood up. "My mother used to call it Double Dips."

"Like ice cream?"

"I guess so. You know, you always want two scoops of the best? And remember: we were being conservative. We only doubled the good things. I'll bet if you really figured out what each of the good ones was worth, you'd find out you didn't just have a good year. You probably had a fantastic year."

She turned the TV back on and walked out.

COOKING

HOME ECONOMICS IS ITS REAL NAME. WE CALL IT HOME ECH.

I don't know if it's Women's Lib or what, but somebody decided that all the boys had to learn how to be little housewives. So now there's coed Home Ech classes. The boys have to learn to sew and decorate and cook. I don't see them teaching the girls how to put a patch on a bike tire or how to survive without a handkerchief.

I just started Home Ech this semester. Cooking is first.

A cooking room is like a combination classroom and kitchen. You walk in and the first thing you see on your right is this big bin full of white stuff. Turns out to be flour. Other bins have other stuff, like sugar. The next wall is a whole row of ovens. Then comes sinks and refrigerators and cabinets. In the middle of all this is a bunch of tables. The back part of the room is where the desks are.

The way it's supposed to work is, you sit down at your desks first, and the teacher tells you how to cook something. Then you get up and go cook.

Our teacher is Miss Perch. She's about ninety-nine years

old and she has pure shiny white hair all in a million tiny rings and she always wears an apron with flowers. One time it's daisies, the next time daffodils. I don't know how tall she was in her prime, but she's practically a midget now. She's way smaller than me. It's weird looking down on a teacher. Her earrings never change.

It's like Miss Perch got lost in the wrong time and place. Sometimes it's hard to believe she knows who she's talking to. She's crazy about cooking. She thinks cooking — and etiquette — are about the most important things in the whole world. She gets all excited about it. Telling us about this breakfast she had on a veranda once. Or how to make gravy without lumps. (Big deal. I always thought lumps were the best part.) Or what a big tragedy it was once when somebody at a fancy dinner ate his salad with a spoon.

If the story she's telling is supposed to be funny, she titters through the whole thing. Or she goes into this big frown — she actually looks heartbroken — if it's about a dish that flopped or bad table manners. And the funny thing is, that even though she really gets into it, she doesn't notice that she's the only one. The rest of us are back there rolling little dough balls or yawning or doing just about anything except listening.

She talks funny too. Not like we're a bunch of junior high school kids, but like we're all hoity-toity grownups nodding and sipping away in some royal tea garden. "Can you imagine!" she's always saying. And "Just a tad, dear." And "Glorious!" And "to-*mah*-to."

No matter what's going on, whether somebody moos in the back row or we're having a chocolate chip fight, she never changes. You get the feeling that when boys first started coming into her class, she never really noticed. I heard that a ninth-grader farted real loud once while she was beating an egg, and she just said "God bless you" and went on beating.

Whatever Miss Perch does, she does it delicate. The grossest thing you'll ever see her do is sweat, and then she dabs her forehead with this little pink tissue she keeps in her apron. When I think of her house I think of a cottage made of doilies and glass birds with thin stem legs. I never saw her sit down.

As far as Miss Perch is concerned, there isn't a morsel of food anywhere in the world that isn't "Glorious!" Not even a crumb. One time she held up an egg and said, "Behold, the egg," and went on talking about it for half the period. You would have thought it was lamb chops or a foot-long hotdog or something.

The first thing she ever had us make was toast and tea. First off she told us about the glories of toast. How heating bread actually makes it sweeter by changing starch to sugar. And how no emperor in history ever ate anything better than a slice of thick homemade toast with fresh-churned butter on it.

Then she made her first mistake: she brought out the tongs. She has these wooden toast tongs for picking out the toast instead of getting your grungy paws on it. Well, all you heard for the rest of the period was squawks from girls who were getting pinched.

As for the tea: no bags. Miss Perch never uses bags. That's low class. You put these loose tea pieces in a silver ball that has holes in it, and then you put that in the hot water. You're supposed to mix different kinds of tea pieces so you get these "exquisite blends." You can have tea a thousand days in a row this way, she says, and never have the same taste twice.

When she heard Linda McDowell scream with delight, she

just swung her head in that direction and smiled. You could tell she figured Linda just discovered an exquisite blend. What she didn't know was that Linda was having her tea leaves read by Grace Lott, who's a little on the weird side and has a second aunt who's a reader and adviser on the board-walk. Linda squealed because Grace just told her that somebody whose name starts with *L* would ask her to the Valentine's dance, and everybody knows Linda has the hots for Larry Delong.

That's how it went just about every class. One time a blender got stuck on HI, and before a janitor came and was brilliant enough to pull out the plug, there was mashed potatoes flying all over the place.

Another time the dough turned green because somebody with dirty hands kneaded it too much.

Another time Bonnie Osteen threw up her own pancakes. She did it because while she was eating them she happened to look across the table and see Eddie Nedich grinning at her. Eddie is known as Nedich the Nosepicker. Most people try to dig their boogies out on the sly. Not Eddie Nedich. His calling cards are all over school. Knowing Eddie is in your Home Ech class, when it comes time to eat what you cooked, you get a little nervous. You have to be very careful. Bonnie Osteen forgot — until she saw him grinning.

Years from now, if you ever visit Avon Oaks Junior High School, you'll know exactly what desks Eddie Nedich the Nosepicker sat in just by running your finger under the seats.

And while I'm on the subject, I have this theory: emeralds are petrified dinosaur snots.

Anyway, I don't think there's ever a class that turns out exactly the way Miss Perch plans it. But you wouldn't know it from her. At the end of each period, there she is at the doorway, like a little old hostess, nodding and smiling and going, "Bon appeteet."

The big event was when Herman the janitor retired. H was there about as long as Miss Perch, and he had to go down to Florida and couldn't wait until the end of the school year. So the teachers (he was everybody's favorite janitor) decided to give him a little farewell party. Miss Perch said we would make the food.

For a couple periods we just talked about the party and great farewell parties of the past. It was going to be all desserts. We would work in pairs.

My partner was Richie.

Calvin is in my class too, and his partner was — of all people — McAllister. The tromboner. It's the first class I ever had with her. She's so goody-goody she makes you feel like Godzilla next to her. You can tell she's Miss Perch's pet: she's the only one whose name Miss Perch remembers.

And she must love Miss Perch too, because Miss Perch calls her Marceline, instead of Marcy. She hates to be called Marcy. Her homeroom teacher did it on the first day of class, and the tromboner goes, "My name is Marceline." So naturally everybody calls her Marcy. The kids anyway.

No eggs smashing at McAllister's feet. Oh no. And you won't find her sticking a carrot in her ear or stomping on a muffin or sneaking some raisins into her pocket. She even goes home and makes some of the things Miss Perch talks about. I stay away from her. One time we were both backing away from stoves with pans of cinnamon buns and we bumped into each other. She sort of looked over her shoulder, like I was a bug, and said, "Excusez-moi."

Strange pair, her and Calvin. I asked him why he picked

her for a partner. He said she asked him. Because none of the girls wanted her, probably. She wouldn't exactly beat Debbie Breen in a popularity contest.

Me and Richie decided we would make fudge for the party. My mother said it was easy. So we were talking about it.

"What kind of fudge we gonna make?" I said.

So we listed the kinds we knew, which were vanilla and chocolate. We voted for chocolate.

"We gonna put anything in it?" I said.

"Like what?" Richie said.

"I don't know," I said. "Nuts, coconut, peanut butter . . ."

Then he said, "Bugs."

That's Richie for you. He's got a weird brain. When there's a question, it just sort of skips right over all the sensible answers and lands on the craziest one. But not so crazy that you don't stop and think about it.

We thought about bugs, and we talked about it, and the more we talked about it the better it sounded. We talked about people eating chocolate-covered ants. And how some guy in the Bible ate locusts. And how the aborigines in Australia eat grubs and stuff. ("Glorious!" I guess Miss Perch would say.) And Richie said there's even bugs in the food we eat. It's just that they get all ground up, and the government says as long as there aren't too many, it's okay. Just for instance, say you have a truckload of spaghetti sauce. Well, maybe the government says it's okay to have a hundred fleas in it, but not a hundred and one. And that's just fleas. The other kinds of bugs get limits too. I don't know who counts them. And anyway, once you cook a bug, it's like anything else: the germs all get killed.

So we figured it wouldn't hurt anybody. And that meant there were no reasons left not to do it.

We forgot one thing though: it was winter. Most of the bugs were gone. All you could get were some inside types. Our house, we have some of these little white spiders, and every once in a while you might see a thousand-legger on the wall. But no way I was getting close enough to catch any of them. It was pretty much the same in Richie's house.

About all that was left was roaches, which neither of us have.

"I bet Dugan's house has 'em," I said.

"Yeah, I bet," said Richie.

Then Richie remembered hearing about this lady who works at the museum of natural history in the city. She decided to see what would happen if you caught a roach, but instead of killing it you gave it all it wanted to eat. He said when he heard about it, the roach was big as a hotdog and still growing.

So much for roaches.

It looked like we were going to have to give up the whole idea. ("Does your sister *really* have cooties?" Richie wanted to know.) Then one day in the middle of science class Richie throws a pencil at me. He's pointing to the back of the room, and before I turn around I know exactly what he's thinking. Right under our noses all the time: *the ant farm.*

The teacher made a big deal out of it the first couple days of school, then everybody pretty much forgot about it. It was pretty neat, you had to admit that. This big tank, all glass, so you could see the ants underground making all their little tunnels and rooms and all. There were a lot of them.

The only problem was hanging around the room long enough after school until we were sure the teacher was gone. We flipped. I lost. Richie stayed lookout at the door. I slid off the cover of the tank and stuck a giant pinwheel taffy in the ground. When some of the ants crawled up onto it, I just took it out and shook it into an empty cole-slaw container. I did it enough times to get about fifty ants. Then I shut the tank, put the container and taffy in my gym bag, and we took off.

We had to work fast. Herman's party was the next day. We went over to Richie's house, because he doesn't have a loudmouth sister or a squealing little brother around. The plan was to fix the ants at Richie's, then do the rest at school. Our class was allowed to take all morning to get the stuff ready.

First thing I did was start to poke tiny holes in the cole slaw container.

"What're you doing that for?" Richie said.

"Let 'em breathe," I told him.

"Why?" he goes. "Aren't we cooking them?"

"Oh, yeah," I said.

So how do you cook an ant? We sure didn't know. It wouldn't be in a book, not in our library anyway. And we couldn't ask anybody.

"Are you sure we have to cook them ahead of time?" I said. "Maybe it's like turkey stuffing. They just cook along with the fudge."

"But you don't cook the fudge," he said, "except to melt the chocolate."

"So, we melt 'em along with the chocolate," I said.

We talked about that for a while. We figured if there's

anything worse than eating an ant, it's eating a *soft* ant. We didn't want the whole party throwing up at once.

"They gotta be crunchy," I said.

"Crispy!" Richie goes. "Like the Colonel's fried chicken. Extra crispy."

"Yeah," I said.

So we figured that left out boiling them. And we couldn't roast them, because we weren't allowed to use the oven. Toasting was out.

"We gotta fry 'em," I said.

"Yeah," Richie said.

So we put on a frying pan.

"High or low?" Richie said.

"Medium," I said. I was starting to feel confident.

"We need butter for frying, right?" he said.

"Nope," I said. "Look." I pointed to the pan.

"What?"

"Teflon. They won't stick. Nothing sticks to Teflon. Don't need butter."

Richie didn't give up. He said bugs have amazingly sticky feet; that's why they can crawl around upside down. "And besides," he goes, "they never tested Teflon on ants."

He had a point. "Yeah," I said, "but if we put butter in, it might keep them soggy."

Then he said, "Yeah, but suppose we don't use butter. And suppose they don't stick. Then they might go flying all over the place. Like grease. We need butter to hold 'em down."

So we argued back and forth. Butter or no butter. Then I happened to look into the pan cabinet, where the door was open, and my eye caught something. "Popcorn popper!"

Richie knew how to use it. He put in some oil, plugged it in, and pretty soon there they were: fifty unsalted, unbuttered, popped ants.

In school the next day everything went great. The only hairy moment came when we dumped in the ants; we had to sort of huddle over the bowl to keep everybody from seeing. When it all hardened we cut it into squares. You could see some of the ants. They looked kind of like pieces of burnt raisins. I was glad we picked chocolate fudge. They would have showed up a lot worse in vanilla.

Miss Perch came by. Her eyebrows went up. Her fingertips went to her chest. "My, my," she goes, "you boys have done a fine fudge, now haven't you? Are samples in order?"

I looked at Richie. He looked at me. I said, "I guess so."

She didn't eat a whole square, just a little piece of one. She worked on it for a while with her eyes closed, her fingertips still on her chest, kind of fluttering like they were thinking about it. Then they stopped. She looked like she was sleeping. Dreaming. Then all her wrinkles went into a smile. Her eyes opened. "Glooorious," she said. "May I ask what is in it?"

"Rice Krispies," I said. "We fried them first. That's why they're black like that."

She walked away nodding and smiling.

Calvin and McAllister made the fanciest thing of anybody. It had about four layers and all different kinds of icing and whip cream and fruit and nuts. They called it a torte. The Waterloo Torte.

"That ain't no torte," I told Calvin. "It's a cake."

"It's a torte," he said.

"Calvin," I said, "don't you know what a cake is?" (For

a microsecond I thought maybe he didn't. Maybe blacks just had pies.) "Cake is cake. You trying to be high society or something?"

"It's a torte."

"How do you know?"

"I saw it in a magazine."

"What magazine?"

"*Gormay.*"

"*Gormay*? What kinda magazine's that?"

"It's about food. People that are experts in eating."

"Where'd you see it?"

"Marceline's."

It figured. Then he asked for a piece of fudge.

"Just a tiny piece," I said. "Miss Perch said to save it for the party."

I broke off a little piece from a corner that I was sure didn't have an ant in it. He liked it.

"Here," I said, "why don't you give a piece to your partner?"

He looked surprised. "Why you giving her something? I thought you didn't like her."

"I don't," I said. "That's why. There's ants in it."

He laughed and took it over. He didn't believe me, like I figured. I didn't actually see him give it to her, but her mouth was working away on something while she was icing the Waterloo Torte.

By the time the party was over, not a piece of fudge was left.

Richie fluttered his fingertips at his chest. "Glorious!"

"Bon appeteet!" I tweeted.

HEARTS

"I'M ONLY GOING FOR THE FOOD," I KEPT TELLING THEM, BUT they wouldn't believe me. Mom kept trying not to grin, and Ham kept saying, "Of course. The food. Why else?"

Well, it was true. I was going to the Valentine's dance because of the free food. Mainly, anyway. Richie came up with the proof. He said: "I can prove we're goin' just mainly for the food."

"How?" I asked him.

"Because even if they were having a class in the gym that night, if they were serving free food, we would still go."

There's your proof.

So, with that out of the way, I could start concentrating on other stuff. Like Debbie Breen, and what to do about her and Valentine's Day. I know one thing: it was time to move up from those second-grade paper hearts and "Guess Who" and "Your Secret Admirer" and "from 10-1-19-15-14."

Things were going pretty good lately. She came the closest yet to coming to my house to see the space station. She said okay, she'd come, and she would have, except at the last minute she had a toothache and had to go to the dentist right away.

And then, when I asked if she was going to the Valentine's dance, she said, "Sure," and then she asked if I was going.

I was cool. I just sort of nonchalanted it and said, "I might."

Afterward I could have killed myself. Why did I say that? If I gave her the impression I wasn't going, maybe she would decide not to go too. She might be thinking I wasn't interested in her anymore.

It was being afraid of the damage that blunder might cause that made me see what I had to do: get her a heart-shaped box of candy.

So I went looking for it with Peter Kim. When it comes to talking about Debbie, it's Peter I feel comfortablest with. Richie knows me too well already. Dugan would only laugh and wisecrack. Calvin wouldn't care. But Peter — I don't know why — I just feel I could say almost anything to him, even embarrassing stuff, and he would take it just right.

We went to the mall. Naturally Peter's little brother Kippy had to come along too. We looked all over: department stores, drugstores, Woolworth's. There were all kinds: little ones, big ones, giant ones, red, purple, white, yellow, ribbons, lace, bows, cupids, flowers. I never knew there were so many kinds of hearts.

I never knew they cost so much, either. I couldn't believe the prices. Those second-grade cards used to be about 5¢ apiece.

"Look how much they cost," I said to Peter. "What do they cost so much for?"

"Must be good candy," he said.

"I only got five dollars."

"I can loan you some."

"That's okay," I said. "I didn't mean that. I just didn't think they would be so much."

"Must be inflation," he said.

I said, "What's inflation got to do with love?" It was the first time I ever remember saying that word out loud. Sure enough, Peter took it in stride.

"How about these?" he said. He was holding up a plastic bag of those little red cinnamon hearts. It cost 59¢.

I just sort of smiled and said no thanks. Just because Peter's a good listener doesn't mean he always understands.

It would have been a lot easier if Kippy wasn't along. Every time we passed a food place he said he had to have some. And Peter would get it for him. Soft pretzel. Hotdog. Giant chocolate chip cookie. (As big as his face. That's what Kippy's flat, round face looks like — a giant cookie. With chocolate chips for eyes.)

I told Peter, "You're spoiling him."

"Why's that?" he said.

"'Cause you're giving him everything he wants. You're not supposed to do that to little kids."

"No? Why not?"

"'Cause then they'll want everything. When they grow up they'll be lazy."

"Not Koreans," he said. "We don't get spoiled."

I laughed. That's Peter's new way of getting back at me for always calling him Korean instead of American. Whenever I criticize him, he calls himself a Korean and says that's the way they are.

Well, I finally picked out a box at Woolworth's. It was on

the small side. Smaller than a baseball glove. The color was the best part: light purple. With a dark purple bow. No cupids or flowers. It was $5 exactly. I let Peter loan me the money for the tax.

Now that I had the heart-shaped candy box, I didn't know how to give it to her. I'm not stupid. I didn't want to make a fool of myself, so there was no way I was going to take it into school.

For days and nights I just dreamed away. Over and over I saw myself giving it to her, and her opening it and squealing with joy and throwing her arms around my neck.

I did a lot of dreaming about the dance too. A million times I said, "Like to dance, Deb?" and a million times she turned and smiled and said, "Love to," and while colored lights swirled and the music played, we danced and danced like the whole gym was ours. We danced some fast ones, and the steps we did were better than on TV, never seen before, and the others — even the ninth-graders — made a circle around us and clapped and whistled and cheered, "Go, Jason! Go, baby!" And we danced slow ones too, long and slow, and our eyes were closed and the dance floor was all music and whispers....

But when Saturday came, the day of the dance, the heart-shaped box was still in the bottom of my drawer beneath my underwear. And when I tried a dance step in front of my mirror, I knew if a dance crowd ever came circling around me, it wouldn't be to cheer.

I went out alone that day. Just to walk. It was cold and bleak and icy. I wished time would stand still. I wanted it to stay the day before the dance forever, so I could always be sure she would throw her arms around my neck, and that when I asked her to dance she would really turn and smile and say, "Love to."

Along the way I saw the Rocksalt Lady. Nobody knows her real name. Or even exactly where she lives. She came toward me, shuffling along in her galoshes, throwing rocksalt from a box out in front of her, so she wouldn't slip on the ice. All winter long, even if it hasn't snowed for a month, you'll never see her without her box of rocksalt. She always dresses the same, winter and summer: the galoshes, a long black coat, and a big green scarf like a monk's hood or something. In the summer the only difference is, she trades in her rocksalt for a shopping bag and goes around picking weeds and dandelions.

Even when she passed right by me, I couldn't see her face. Nobody ever did. Except Dugan said he did once. We don't know if it's true, but if anybody would, he would. He said he just planted himself right in front of her one day and turned his head sideways and gawked right up into the green hood. He said it looked like a paper bag in there, when you crumple and crinkle it all up.

I got a strange feeling when the Rocksalt Lady went by. Even after she passed, it was like she still wasn't gone. I kept hearing the rocksalt falling behind me, like a tiny hailstorm, and ahead of me my feet kept crunching on it. Finally I crossed the street.

Standing around at the dance later that night, I still didn't know what I was going to do.

As soon as we got there I told the guys I was going to the bathroom. What I really did was go outside and hide the heart-shaped candy box under a bush. All the way walking to the dance, I had it safety-pinned by the purple ribbon to the lining on the inside back of my coat.

It's scary walking to your first dance. I wouldn't have done it by myself, free food or not. Calvin, Richie, Peter Kim, me — we all walked together. Dugan didn't go with us. He just showed up later. Alone, as usual. Dugan is scared of absolutely nothing. Nothing. For the first and only time in my life, I was actually a little sorry Kippy wasn't along.

Along the way we did a lot of messing around and laughing and moosecalling. But not a word about the dance. On our insides I think we all felt like it was the last long walk to the gallows. I half expected to look over and see this little old padre walking along with us mumbling verses out of the Bible.

When we got there we just trucked on by the gym doors. It was bad enough hearing the music and just feeling it so close. Nobody was ready to actually look, much less go in. So everybody headed for the food, which is when I ducked out to hide the candy box.

The food — all this great free food that we said we were coming for — turned out to be sodas, in teeny-weeny paper cups, and pretzels. A couple of ugly ninth-graders were serving. But nobody wanted to admit how junky it was, so we hung and hung and hung around the food table until we got kicked away.

Finally there was nothing left to do but go into the dance. There was twisted crepe paper swooping down from all parts of the ceiling and meeting right over the center of the court. And coming down from there was this humongous red heart, hanging pretty low, and pasted onto it were all these little white hearts.

The eighth- and ninth-graders—especially the ninth-graders—sort of dominated the place. It was like they were the lions at the waterhole: they hogged up all the good spots. The head lions were The Lovers. They just stuck under the hanging heart, leaning a little bit this way and that to the music. All that was left for us little seventh-grade rodents were some puddles on the side. From where we were we could see some of the ninth-graders writing on the little white hearts that were on the big red one.

"They're writing their names. 'Somebody Loves Somebody.' Stuff like that," Dugan told us. Before we ever came in, Dugan had already been to the middle of the floor. Not dancing, of course. Just checking things out.

It was Dugan that noticed we still had our coats on. We laughed as we took them off. We laughed so hard we almost went into convulsions.

We moved around the place the way you cross a creek. You stand on a good rock, and you don't move until you spot the next rock. It has to be another good one, that's big and steady enough to hold you, and not too far away. When you spot one like that, that's when you take your next step. Only in the gym, instead of rocks there were little knots of seventh-graders. Especially guys that we knew.

We would slap hands and say something about the scrimpy food and school and basketball and how we had to get dressed up to come. After a while, though, what we did more and more was play a new game. It's called Who's That One.

All the girls were in dresses. With high heels. The first thing it made you think of was church. Most of their hair was different too. I guess the combination of that and the darkness made it hard to tell who was who. So you'd see this girl go wobbling past with this dress on and fancy hairdo and you'd say, "Who's that one?"

There were only about two that you could recognize right off: Marceline (Don't-Call-Me-Marcy) McAllister and Esther Kufel. McAllister had a dress on, all right, but other than that she didn't exactly kill herself trying to look beautiful. Same hair. Same no-makeup. Esther Kufel — well, she always looks like she just got out of bed. Esther's kind of retarded, but they're allowed in regular schools these days. She talks like there's something in her mouth. Her glasses are so thick they're like old-fashioned Coke bottles. It looked like her and the tromboner came together.

Gorgeous. That's what Debbie Breen was. She had a blue dress on, and her hair was kind of fluffed up on top of her head, except for a couple little ringlets that came spilling down the sides. She still flicked her head once in a while, even though no hair was in her eye. I got all queasy whenever she did it.

No matter where we were or what we were doing, I always kept an eye on her. Like radar. I knew she came with her girlfriends, and she did a lot of dancing with them, but guys kept going over to ask her to dance too. She acted nice and friendly to all of them. She smiled all over the place and flicked her head. Different guys went over. She wasn't attached to anybody. That's one thing I knew.

The only ones that gave me a hard time about her were Richie and Dugan. Richie wasn't too bad. He just kept saying stuff like, "Wow! Look at *that* one!" And, "Man, you sure know how to pick 'em."

But Dugan, he was hard-core. He's the type of person that,

what everybody else might only think, he'll say. Like, "Hey, ain't that that Breen girl? Who's that she's dancin' with?" And, "Hey Herk, whydn't you go ask her to dance?"

The worst thing, though, was him saying he would go ask her to dance *for* me. "Hey Herk," he kept going, "I'll get a dance for ya." He kept getting more and more ballsy about it. At first he just took a step or two in her direction, then wheeled around and came back. Then he kept going farther and farther, getting closer and closer to her before he wheeled around. I knew he was waiting for me to make an ass of myself by calling him out loud to stop.

Then one time he made up his mind to go all the way. I could just tell. "I'll getcha a dance," he said and he was gone. He headed over to the little group of girls where she was. He was going to do it, no question he was going to do it. Dugan didn't care. He loves to embarrass people. He was heading straight for her — her back was toward him — his arm was going up — he was going to tap her on the shoulder — "*Dugan!*" I hollered — and he strolled on behind her, scratching his head. By the time the girls finished turning to see who had the big mouth, I was already melted back into the crowd.

Most of the guys that were going over and asking Debbie to dance were ninth-graders. And most were tall ones. Any one of them could have been the other Luke Skywalker. When one of them would take her out to the dance floor, her girlfriends turned and grabbed each other's arms and whispered and giggled. I kept thinking of the purple candy box out under the bush.

Then I saw her head out to the food table. It was now or never. I said I had to go to the bathroom and left. All night long I was working on something to say to her. I figured I had just the right line. It would remind her of past times, and it would kind of bring her back to me.

She was at the table, picking up a soda. All of a sudden I didn't like the glare of the lights. I wanted to check in a mirror. It was kind of like feeling your fly was open on your face.

But there wasn't time. I went to the table, sort of wedged in next to her, grabbed a soda, turned, and acted surprised to be bumping into her.

"Hi," I said.

She smiled at me. "Hi. Thought you weren't coming."

That was a good sign. She remembered — sort of — what I had said. "I said I *might* come."

"Oh, that's right," she said.

Time for the line. I picked up a pretzel. I held in in front of her. I frowned at it. I said, "Not exactly a marshmallow, huh?"

She laughed. "Or a hotdog."

"Hey," I said, "you just get here? I didn't see you around."

I handed her the pretzel. She took it, took a bite. "We were here for a while," she said. White pretzel specks came out. I wanted to take a shower in them.

"Been dancin'?" I said.

She shrugged. "A little, I guess." She was looking, squinting at the lights.

"Well," I said. I grabbed another pretzel and backed off. I didn't want to be too close in case the answer was bad. "Gotta save me a dance, okay?"

She crunched on her pretzel. "Okay," she said. "Sure."

I sailed back into the gym. It seemed all comfortable and

friendly now. I went right across the middle of the floor, right past the big red hanging heart. A little voice inside me was humming: *Okay, she said. Sure, she said. Okay, she said.*

Then it all started to fall apart.

First, it took a couple songs before Debbie came back into the gym.

Then a couple more before I got up the nerve to walk over to her.

And then, just when I was ready, the supercool ninth-grader who was acting as the DJ announces: "Okay, all you dudes. Stand back and watch out for your Valentines, 'cause it's a *dudettes' choice!!*"

I sort of slid over to the dance-floor side of the group of guys I was with, so I'd be easy to find. But I kept talking so I wouldn't look like I was expecting or hoping for anything.

The song started. It was a slow one. I could see the guys being led away from the sidelines by girls that asked them. My mouth kept jabbering to the guys, but inside I was praying for a tap on the shoulder, a sweet marshmallow voice to say, "Jason? Like to dance?"

The song went on. I couldn't not look forever. I turned. I sniffed. I put on my bored look. I yawned. I saw her. Out under the big red heart. With a ninth-grader. She just about came up to his armpit. Her free arm had to go practically straight up to hook around his neck. His nose was down in her hair. Her face was up in his Adam's apple. She was on tiptoes even in her high heels. You couldn't squeeze a fart between them.

Then all of a sudden I hear Dugan's voice: "Oh no, not me!"

I turn. Dugan is shaking his head and pretending to limp. Esther Kufel is standing in front of him. Just as soon as I look over, Dugan sees me and he points and goes, "Him. Jason wanted to ask ya."

I took off. Just as I was turning I caught a glimpse of Marceline McAllister in the background, watching it all.

I went outside. I wanted to swear, cry, scream, spit, kick, and kill myself — anybody — all at once. I cursed ninth-graders. I cursed Debbie Breen. I cursed dances. I cursed my mother and father for making me short. I cursed girls. I looked around. Nobody was there. "Here ya go!" I yelled, and I gave the world the finger.

I walked around the school. My breath came out in clouds, but I didn't even feel the cold. I just kept muttering: "Shit. Shit. Horse shit. Dog shit. Monkey shit. Pig shit. Shit shit."

I told Debbie Breen what I'd do with the marshmallow stick if she ever came around me again at a hayride. I told her her face would have to be my sofa for a year before she ever got an invitation to see my space station again. I told her the next time she saw a football game she'd see me score five touchdowns, then be carried off the field to the waiting arms of the captain of the ninth-grade varsity cheerleaders.

As if it wasn't bad enough to feel rotten about the rest of the world, I had to feel rotten about myself too. I could picture the Perfect Miss McAllister back in there, deciding what a cruel rat I was. It's true I didn't *want* to dance with Esther Kufel, and it's true I was glad I got out of it. But it's also true that I felt bad about it. I do have feelings, and I do try to be aware of other people's feelings and not hurt them. But Miss Perfect didn't know that. She probably figured I was just like Dugan. She was already gone from the vice-principal's office when Ham told him: "He's a good kid."

You know you're really in a bad way when the best thing that happened to you was not having to dance with a retard —and you can't even feel good about *that*. I couldn't even go home. As soon as I opened the door Ham would go, "Well, how was the food?"

I wished somebody would come along with a gun and put me out of my misery.

I was back at the dance door. Esther Kufel was standing there. She was alone. She must have been waiting for McAllister.

I didn't think. I just talked. Fast. "Esther, hi. Listen. I was just talking to some guy—this is no joke, believe me—I was talking to this guy and he says he was kinda shy and didn't want to come in to the dance, know what I mean? But he said—swear to God—he said he brought you a box of candy and he hid it—for *you*—out under the bush that's right next to the boys main entrance. Know where that is?"

She didn't seem to know. I was getting nervous. I started moving in toward the gym. "Ask Marceline," I said. "Bush by the boys door. Purple Box. Purple ribbon. Honest to God."

In the gym there was an uproar of screams and squeals. Somebody pulled down the big red heart, and now all the curlicued red and white crepe paper was floating down from the ceiling all over everybody.

SPRING

THE AIR FEELS LIKE BASEBALL.

It's light out after dinner.

It rains and the worms come out onto the sidewalks to be squashed by the millions.

The cops caught a guy running naked down some street.

I don't hate Debbie Breen anymore. I write letters to her that I never mail. They say, "I will keep on loving you even though you like other guys. I will love you forever. Someday you will cry and remember and you will reach out and claw some furniture and cry out, *My God! Why didn't I marry Jason Herkimer?*"

I don't feel like sitting in school.

There's a lot of new stuff in the gutters and sewer grates.

The Rocksalt Lady is carrying her shopping bag now.

The ground is spongy. Sometimes it smells like onions.

As the leaves come out, the birds' nests disappear.

Ham bought three bags of dried cow dung for the vegetable garden. He's all excited about it.

The little kids are back out on the corner. They had paper ready for me to make them airplanes.

I opened a window and didn't get hollered at.

My mother moved the geranium from the dining room to the porch and hung her bathing suit outside.

I washed my bicycle. A bird pooped on it.

I peed in a parking lot.

MOTHERS

I couldn't find my baseball glove. And that was impossible. Every year in the fall I put my glove on the shelf in my bedroom closet, and in the spring I take it out. That's just the way it is. It snows in the winter, the leaves turn colors in the fall, and in the spring I reach up to the shelf and pull down my baseball glove.

Only it wasn't there.

"It's always there," I told Calvin. "Always."

I kept feeling around with my hand. I got up on a chair and looked. No glove.

"Timmy stole it," I said. I yelled: "Timmy!"

"Stop yelling like that. He's out," came my mother's voice from downstairs.

"I'll kill him," I said.

Calvin said, "Why would he take it?"

"Who knows?" I growled. "Maybe he's tired of stealing my dinosaurs." I kicked the chair across the room. It rammed into the bureau.

"Jason!" from downstairs.

"Your mother's gonna kill you before you kill your brother," Calvin informed me.

"Funny," I said.

"It's around someplace," he said. "Why's it so important anyway?"

How could I answer that? If I told the whole truth I'd have to say: It's important because I wanted to show off, Calvin. I wanted to show you that I'm serious about baseball. Not like you guys. I want to show you how I rub oil into it after the baseball season; and it's gotta be *olive* oil. Because that keeps the glove from drying out and cracking, and it keeps the leather tender so it can feel the ground balls just right. And then — see? — after I oil it I put a baseball into it and curl the fingers over it. That's for the pocket. A glove's nothing without a good pocket. It's gotta be deep. Then see how I wedge it into this small shoe box so it'll stay curled. And that's how it stays all winter long. There's a lot to keeping a glove. And I can't tell you about it. I have to show you.

How could I say all that? So I just said, "It's important, that's all."

He asked me if I was going out for the school team this year.

"Sure," I said. "Why not?"

"Think you'll make it?"

"I got a chance."

"What're you goin' out for?"

I snarled at him. "Waddaya think?"

That's the kind of thing that makes me mad. Calvin knows I'm a shortstop. Everybody knows I'm a shortstop. I played it in Little League. Even in our pickup games at the park, it's the only position I ever play.

"It's not Little League, y'know," he tells me.

"Yeah, Calvin, so I heard. Say, Calvin, anyway, wha'd *you* hit in Little League last year?" My batting average was almost .330. Calvin hit a blockbuster .265.

"Who cares?" he goes. "I ended my baseball career last year. I'm retired."

"You didn't retire, Calvin. You gave up."

"You still gonna be a major leaguer?" His eyes were snickering.

"I never said I *was*. I said I *might try*."

"Well?"

"I toldja. I might. *Might*."

To myself I was thinking, *I will. Will.* I didn't want to be a major league shortstop all the time. But in the spring, when I felt the air and took my glove out of the box and slipped my fingers into it and took a deep whiff of that soft brown leather, it was the only thing I wanted to be.

While we're doing all this talking, I'm charging from room to room upstairs, jerking out drawers, looking under beds, searching closets. The more I didn't find it the more desperate I got. I was a madman. I didn't bother to put things back. One thing I grabbed (it looked like an old, brown, crinkly Christmas wreath) I sent sailing into a wall like a Frisbee.

Everywhere I looked: no glove.

We went downstairs. Started looking there.

Suddenly I heard my mother shriek upstairs. I heard her stomping overhead, then on the steps. "Jason!" I was surprised she let herself yell like that with somebody else in the house.

I went into the living room. She was stopped halfway

down the stairs. She was holding the ratty old wreath in her hand.

"Huh?" I said.

"What were you *doing* up there?" she goes.

"I was looking for my glove. I can't find it. I always keep it on the shelf in my closet."

"Why were you in *my* closet?" She was still yelling. Her nostrils were red.

"I said. For my glove."

"Why *my* closet?"

"I don't know. I just looked everywhere."

"Looked?" she howled. "You didn't just look! You bashed things around!"

I told her I was sorry. I didn't tell her she was overreacting a little.

"Sorry doesn't do it," she said. "You don't go treating other people's things like your own junk." She shoved out her hand. "You know what this is?"

I said, "A Christmas wreath."

She screeched. "Christmas wreath!"

"Antique Christmas wreath?"

"It's my crown," she said.

"Crown? For what?"

"It's what I wore when I was queen of the ninth-grade prom."

We just stared at each other for a while. Eyes wide. Mouths open. Like we were a couple of goldfish gaping at each other from separate bowls.

When she talked again her voice was almost a whisper. She looked confused. "Why did you throw it against the wall?"

"I don't know," I said. "I didn't know what it was."

We both sort of looked at it. She turned it over, and one of the little brown flaky leaves came loose and fell to the living room rug. I couldn't imagine my mother a queen. She stood on stairways, like now, with a long old shirt of Ham's on and jeans and bare feet. That was my mother.

After a while she turned slow and went up the stairs. I think she was saying, "Please don't throw it against the wall anymore."

Calvin made me go over to his house. He said his glove was all beat up and flat and dried out and he wanted me to fix it up for him.

"I thought you retired from baseball," I reminded him.

"Organized ball," he said. "I'm still gonna be an amateur."

So I went. He was probably trying to patch up what just happened. I was really embarrassed he had to hear all that.

On the way over he said, "My mother was a queen too."

"Yeah?" I said. "What of?" He didn't know. "She got a crown?" He didn't know that either.

When we got to his house his mother was in the kitchen. She was stirring something on the stove with a wooden spoon. It smelled like chili, which I love. I asked her what it was.

"Chili," she said. "I make it for Calvin. He loves it."

"Everybody *but* me loves it," Calvin scowled. "I hate it."

Counting that night for hot chocolate, this was the second time I was in Calvin's kitchen, and I hadn't seen any soul food yet. Being there reminded me of one of the oldest questions in my head: *What are chitlins, anyway?*

I kept watching Mrs. Lemaine at the stove. She had gold

hoop earrings on. Her fingernails and toenails were painted the same color. She was good-looking. Darn good-looking, actually.

Calvin got his glove. He was right about how bad it was. It's a crime to treat a glove that way.

I asked for olive oil.

"How about vegetable oil?" Mrs. Lemaine said.

I told her it had to be olive.

She looked into her cabinet. "Peanut oil?"

"Nope."

"Well," she sighed, "that's all we have. Unless you two want to stomp on these olives."

I thought it over and decided to forget my pride and do it as a favor for Calvin. "Okay," I said. "I'll try the peanut." Besides, Calvin wouldn't know the difference anyway. Or care.

I worked on the glove, and we both munched on crackers. All of a sudden Calvin goes, "You were a queen, weren't you, Mom?"

"Still am," she said, stirring.

Calvin shook his head and shuffled, "C'mon. You know what I mean. What was that thing you were queen of? School, was it?"

She nodded slow. "M-hm."

"What? High school?"

"M-hm."

"The prom?"

She shook her head no. The gold hoops swayed in the steam from the pot.

"What then?"

"The May."

"The May?" goes Calvin, scowling over at me. "What's that?"

"Queen of the May," she said, stirring slow.

"May Queen," I said.

Calvin whispered, "See? Toldja." He turned back to his mom. "Jason's mother was a queen too."

"Oh?" she said.

I was getting a little nervous.

"Yeah," he said. "She was a prom queen."

"I see."

"Hey, Mom, do you still have your crown?"

She stopped stirring. "Nope, 'fraid not." She came toward us. "Okay now, clear out, you guys. I have to set up for dinner. You staying, Jason?"

I told her no thanks, I had to go home. I finished Calvin's glove and left. For some reason I was glad the conversation ended there.

It turned out my glove was at the shoemaker's. One of the seams in the thumb was coming apart, and Ham said a long time ago that when baseball was ready to start again he would take it to a shoemaker to get it repaired. I forgot all that.

It was almost a week later when Calvin told me what happened after I left that day. He said he kept pestering his mom about being May Queen and all — you could tell how proud he was — and so finally she took him into her bedroom and opened up a drawer and took out a rock and handed it to him. He said she told him there were a lot of blacks at her school, but even more whites. He said after she got picked queen there were some bad letters and phone calls. He said they had this little parade, and she was sitting up on the back of a convertible waving away at the people, when somebody threw this rock and it hit her in the head. Knocked her crown off. The rock fell onto the seat. The rock and the crown were both sitting there. She saved the rock. She said she wished now she saved the crown too. Calvin said it was a pretty big rock.

I used to think being a queen was something great.

MILES

I DIDN'T MAKE THE BASEBALL TEAM.

The coach said he already had a ninth-grader for short-stop, and an eighth-grade second-stringer, and I wasn't quite good enough to beat them out. I said I'd be willing to play another position. He said he had veteran ninth-graders at all the positions. I told him I wanted to be a major leaguer someday. I told him I hit almost .330 in Little League last year. He looked impressed. He said that's the kind of spirit he likes to see. He said it's not that I don't have the talent, it's just that I need another year to grow. To mature. In the meantime, he said, he wants me to stay in shape. He said he'd like to see me go out for track. It'd be good for me, he said, and nobody gets cut from track.

I tried out for the sprints. I figured that would help me be a better base-stealer. But I was too slow for the sprints.

I tried the half mile. It was too long to run full speed, and too short to run slow. I couldn't figure it out.

That's how I became a miler.

At first I wasn't too excited about it. I didn't see how

running the mile was going to help me be a better shortstop. I was only doing it because the baseball coach was grooming me for next year.

Then I saw a mile race on TV. Some great miler from England was running, and as he finished each lap the announcer was screaming: "He's on a record pace! He's on a record pace!" Each lap the people in the stands went crazier. On one side of the screen they showed the world record time, and on the other side they showed the runner's time. The whole stadium was standing and screaming, like they were pushing him with their voices, and even though it was the last lap, instead of going slower he was going *faster*. I couldn't believe it. The stadium was going bananas, and he was flying and the world record time and his time were getting closer and closer and he broke the world record by 3/10 of a second. And even then he didn't collapse, or even stop. He just kept jogging another lap around the track, holding his arms up and smiling and waving to the cheering crowd.

Even though it was Saturday, I went outside and ran ten times around the block.

I turned out to be a pretty rotten miler. We had our first time trials, and I came in dead last. My time was 6 minutes and 47 seconds. The guy that broke the world record did it in less than 3 minutes and 50 seconds.

To top it off, I threw up afterward.

And to top that off, the place where I threw up happened to be the long-jump pit. Which didn't make the long jumpers too happy, but which the coach thought was just fine. He said now they had a good reason to jump farther than ever.

But all that, it was nothing. It was all just peaches and cream compared to the worst part, the really, *really* bad thing: one of the people that beat me was named Marceline McAllister. The girl.

"I'm quittin'," I told Peter Kim, who was on the track team too. A half-miler.

"Why?" he said.

"*Why?* You see who I lost to in the time trials?"

"I wasn't watching."

"The girl."

"Which one?" he said. There're other ones on the team too, but she's the only miler one.

"McAllister," I said.

"Marceline?"

"Yeah. Her."

"The one that plays the trombone?"

"Yeah."

He shrugged. "So?"

"So?" I hollered. "Waddaya mean, so? She's a girl, man! You ever lose to a girl?"

He said maybe I had a cramp.

"I didn't have no cramp."

"Maybe you just had a bad day."

"So what?" I screeched. "How bad could it be? She's still a girl. I got beat by a girl. I'm quittin'."

Then he started talking to me. He reminded me that some of the other girls on the team were doing better than last too. In fact, one of them was the second-fastest sprinter in the one-hundred-pound class. He said he heard that at our age a lot of girls are better than boys, because they mature faster. He said in another couple years I'd probably beat her easy.

And he reminded me that the baseball coach had his eye on me.

"Yeah," I said, "he's really gonna be impressed, watching me lose to a girl."

"He didn't tell you to beat anybody," Peter said. "He just said to keep in shape."

I tried to explain. "Peter, all that stuff doesn't make any difference. The thing is, she's a girl. And a girl's a girl. You know what I'm saying? A *girl*. G-I-R-L. You understand me?"

Peter's expression changed. "No," he said, "I don't understand. I'm Korean, remember? Do what you want." He turned and left.

"Okay," I said. "I won't quit." He kept walking. I called, "Just don't tell Dugan! Peter? Hear? Don't tell anybody!"

It was a long, long track season.

Every day we started with calisthenics. Then most days we ran around the whole school grounds. *Five* times. Some other days we did intervals. That's where you run real fast as hard as you can for a while, then walk for a while (a littler while), then run fast again. Run-walk-run-walk. You just listen for the whistle to tell your legs when to start or stop. You'll never know how cruel a whistle is until you're walking after your tenth interval, and you hear it blow again.

As much as I hated practice, there was one good thing about it: you weren't running *against* anybody. There were no places. No first. No last.

That's why I dreaded the first meet. Ham wanted to know when it was.

"Why?" I asked him.

"Mom and I thought we'd like to come see it."

"See me lose?" I said. I didn't tell them about the girl. "I toldja I'm just running to keep in shape for baseball."

"We just like to come and see you, that's all," he said. "We came to all your Little League games, didn't we?"

"That was different. I'm good at baseball."

"We don't care," he said. "We don't come to see you be a star. Just to play."

"Well, anyway," I said, "the meet's away."

Which was true. It was at Mill Township. I came in last. By a lot. But the thing was, it didn't really bother me. That's because on the bus over to the meet I all of a sudden realized something: even though I was running, I wasn't really in the *race*. If all I was supposed to be doing was staying in shape for baseball, there was no use getting all uptight about where I finished. I was actually running for the baseball coach, not the track coach. I was a baseball player disguised as a track runner. I didn't really want to break the world's record. I was no miler. I was a shortstop.

It was a big relief when I thought about all that. It still might look to some people like I was losing to a girl. But inside I knew the truth. You can't lose if you're not racing.

After the mile the coach called to me. "Herkimer? You okay?"

"Yeah," I said. I was still jogging. I was hardly puffing. I thought I'd do another couple laps around the grass. Really get in shape.

"Hold it," he said. He came over. "Nothing wrong? Muscle pull? Dizzy?"

"Nah," I told him. "I'm okay."

He looked at me funny. "So why were you taking it so easy?"

I told him the whole thing, which to be fair I probably

should have done the first day of practice. I told him about the baseball coach. About being groomed for next year. About wanting to be a major league shortstop.

He was nodding his head while I said these things. When I finished, he still kept nodding, looking at me. Then he stopped. He bent over so his face was right opposite mine. He didn't blink. His voice was hoarse. Almost a whisper.

"What's your first name?"

"Jason."

"Jason? Jason, when you're on my team, you run. And you run as well as you can. I don't care if you're slower than a turtle, you'll try your best when you're on my team. You will run as hard as you can. Every step of the way. Do you understand?"

I nodded.

"And next time I see you dogging it, you are no longer on my team. Understood?"

I understood.

So much for taking it easy.

So I did my calisthenics and ran my five times around the school and did my intervals and I tried harder.

In the second meet I brought my time down to 6:30. I was still last. McAllister's time was 6:15.

In the next couple meets I kept improving. But so did she. Our best miler, Floatmeier, a ninth-grader, only talked to me once. He said, "When you gonna beat that girl?" I tried. But by the middle of the season she was still a good ten seconds faster.

Ham kept asking about the meets. I kept telling him they were away. After a while he got the idea and stopped asking.

Then something happened that made me try even harder.

We were racing Shelbourne, and they had a girl miler too — and *she* beat me.

The next day at practice I ran around the school six times. I did my calisthenics perfectly. Even after fifteen intervals I dared that whistle to blow again.

Next meet, for the first time, I didn't come in last. I beat somebody. A kid on the other team.

Peter saw I was trying harder. He started running with me at practice. (He takes track seriously, like I take baseball.) During my races he would stand at the last turn with a stop-watch, and at each lap he would call out my time and yell, "Go, Jason! Go! Go!" And on the last lap, coming off the final turn, he would yell at me, "Sprint! Now! All out! Sprint! Now! Now!" And he would be sprinting along on the grass with me.

My times got better. I broke the six-minute barrier with a 5:58. (In the meantime Floatmeier was running in the 4:50's.) McAllister kept getting better too. I was closing the gap on her, but the closer I got, the harder it got.

Then, on the next-to-last meet of the season, going down the backstretch, I got closer to McAllister than ever before. I was so close I could feel little cinder specks that her spikes were flipping back. Her hands were tight fists. Her hair was flapping like mad from side to side and slapping her in the neck. I could hear her breathing. She was kind of wheezing. Grunting. And all of a sudden, right there on the backstretch, it came to me: *Marceline McAllister wasn't faster than me.* Not really. She was just trying harder. She was trying so hard it scared me.

After practice one day, one of the ninth-graders — a slow ninth-grader — grabbed me outside the girls locker room and dragged me inside. He wouldn't let me out till I read what was on the wall: "McAllister sucks trombones."

"See?" he sneered. "Even the girls don't like her."

I practiced hard in the days before the final meet. But not super hard. The problem wasn't in my legs. It was in my head. I knew I could beat her now, but I didn't know if I wanted to pay the price. And the price was pain. I found that out following her down the backstretch that day. I was really hurting. My legs felt like they were dragging iron hooks through the cinders. My head was flashing and thundering. But the worst part of all was my chest. It felt like somebody opened me up and laid two iron shotputs inside me, one on top of each lung, and each time I breathed out, the shotputs flattened the lungs a little more. By the last one hundred yards there was only about a thimbleful of air to suck from.

When I remembered all that pain, and realized it would have to get even worse for me to go faster, I wasn't sure beating her was worth it. I felt like somebody, somewhere, double-crossed me. I couldn't believe I would have to try so hard just to beat a girl.

The day before the meet, Floatmeier gave me a little punch in the shoulder. "Last chance," he said.

When they called the milers to the start, me and McAllister, as usual, being seventh-graders and the slowest, lined up at the back of the pack. Only this time somebody else lined up with us. It was Pain. He was grinning. *O-h-h-h shit*, I thought. I swore right there this would be the last race I ever ran in my life.

In all my other races, what I did was stay pretty far behind McAllister for the first two or three laps. That way I could save my energy and sprint after her on the last lap. But this time I stuck with her right from the start. Like a wart.

By the end of the first lap I was already blowing hard. My legs were getting a little heavy. Pain didn't touch me yet, but he was right beside me, still grinning. We were really smoking.

We kept it up the second lap. Didn't slow down at all. Her spikes were practically nicking my knees. Our breathings had the same rhythm.

At the half-mile mark things started to get a little scary. Never before, this far into the race, were we this close to the leaders. I was almost as tired already as I usually was at the end of a whole mile. Something had to give. Pain was right there, stride for stride, grinning away. Something was going to happen.

It did. Coming off the first turn into the backstretch of the third lap. The leaders started to go faster. McAllister speeded up too. She was trying to stay with them. *Jesus!* I thought. *She's crazy!*

I had no choice. I had to go too. I stepped on it, and all of a sudden Pain wasn't alongside me anymore. He was *on* me. He was beating up on my head. He was pulling on my legs. He speared a cramp into my side. He opened up my chest and dumped in those two iron shotputs.

Little by little McAllister pulled away: three yards . . . five yards . . . ten yards. . . . When she leaned into the far turn I got a side view of her. She was running great. Long strides. Arms pumping. Leaning just a little forward. Keeping her form. Everything the coach told us.

A feeling I never expected in a million years came over me: I admired her. I was proud of her. I knew she was hurting too, maybe even as bad as me, but there she was, gaining on the guy in front of her. I wanted to be like her.

The gun went off: last lap. Four hundred forty more yards and my racing career would be over.

I reached out, like my own breath was a twisted rope, and pulled myself along. My lungs sagged under the shotputs. I tried to forget that. I shook my arms to relax. *Stride long. Head steady. Keep your form....*

I don't know whether she slowed down or I got faster, but the gap between us closed: ten yards ... five yards ... three yards.... We were on the final backstretch, and I was where I started, nipping at her heels. *Now!* I thought. I pulled alongside her. Floatmeier and some others were already sprinting for the tape, but we were in our own private race, crunching down the cinders, gasping like asthmatics, side by side. We never turned to look at each other.

Then, going into the final turn, she started to edge ahead. A couple inches. A couple feet. I went after her. My lungs disappeared. Only the shotputs now. And now they were doing something. They were getting warm. They were getting hot. They were burning.

I caught her coming off the final turn. Side by side again. There was no form now. No nice fresh strides. With every step we staggered and knocked into each other like cattle coming down a chute. I wished I had the shotputs back, because in my chest now was something worse: two balls of white-hot gas. *Stars!* A pair of stars in my chest. A billion degrees Centigrade. And they were expanding. Exploding. Searing hot star gas scalding into my stomach and arms and legs, into my head. My eyes were star gas. Faces on the side lurched and swayed. The track wobbled under my feet.

Elbows, shoulders, hips colliding. If Peter was running with me I didn't know it. I couldn't see. I couldn't hear. I couldn't breathe. I was dying.

I don't know when I crossed the finish line. I only know they stopped me and held me up and dragged me around with my arms draped over their shoulders.

Somebody came over and slapped me on the back. "Way to go!"

It was Floatmeier's voice.

"Why?" I gasped.

"You beat her, man!"

I opened my eyes. Floatmeier was grinning and holding out his hand. I was too weak to slap it. I sort of petted it.

Then there were hands coming down from everywhere. I did my best to hit them all. "Way to go, Herk," they kept saying. "Way to gut it . . . Way to run . . . Good race . . . Good race . . . Good race . . ."

Finally I plopped to the ground. Little by little I got my shoes off. My chest was returning to normal. The star gas must have gone out through my eyes: they were burning.

Another hand, palm up, in front of me. I slapped it. I looked from the hand to the face. It was McAllister. She looked sick. Her lips were bluish and wet and her mouth was crooked. But then it smiled.

"Good race," she said.

FREEDOM, BASEBALL, BUGS, LINT

School's out!

No more seventh-grader. Let the ninth-graders wipe their feet somewhere else. Now I'm *somebody*.

When I come out of school on the last day, I always run smack into the same problem. It's the problem people have at a smorgasbord, where there's a million things to eat and they don't know where to start. Or sitting in front of a pile of Christmas presents, and you don't know which one to open first. So every year I step out into that warm sunshine, with moosecalls all around and the summer vacation stretching out of sight, and there in front of me are all these goodies, all these things to do, places to go, all the stuff I dreamed about and wished for during the last long nine months of school and winter and homework.

So what do I do? Nothing. I don't know where to start. I go home and sit around. I have a little black-and-white TV in my room. I lie there on my bed and watch it. Game shows. Soap operas even. I close my eyes and go to sleep. I get something to eat. In the first couple days of vacation

186

I don't use much of the world. Or even the house. Mainly I live at two points: the refrigerator and my bed.

Of course that doesn't make Ham too happy — the refrigerator part, that is. He starts to notice the food going faster than during the winter. He notices the refrigerator seems warmer and the motor runs more because the door is open so much.

What gets him madder than anything is finding somebody's been into his ice cream. He has this favorite flavor. Dutch chocolate almond. It doesn't seem fair that he gets a half-gallon all to himself, while the rest of us just get one to split. And we let him know about it. He always says: "Look at all the things you kids get that I don't. Look at all the things that I like that Mom can't make me for dinner because you kids don't like them. I'm forty-one years old. I work hard. I support my family. I've been getting this ice cream for the last twenty years. Long before you kids were born. I do not believe that when I decided to marry your mother I gave up my right to have my ice cream. It costs two dollars and seventy-nine cents, and that's the only money I spend on myself all week. I'm forty-one years old."

I'm not saying I don't agree. It's just that sometimes I like to hang around him when he's eating his Dutch chocolate almond and he knows our half-gallon has been gone for days. I kind of put on my hungry-dog face and try to make him feel guilty. Just so he'll give the speech.

Even then, sometimes his ice cream still disappears when he's not around. Not much of it. Maybe just a spoonful. But he must memorize the exact shape of his ice cream each day, because he says he can tell if any's missing. Then he hollers. But nobody confesses. It's a mystery.

But this year — no hollering, no speech. Not the usual speech anyway. A different one. On freedom.

He comes into my room about noon (his summer-school teaching didn't start yet) and he sees me on the bed, leaning on the pillow, eating a raspberry licorice stick, the fan next to the TV blowing in my face (he doesn't know it, but I'm daydreaming about me and Debbie Breen), and he goes, "The Grand Inquisitor was right."

I said, "Huh?"

"The Grand Inquisitor," he says. "A character in a book. Know what he says?"

"Nope." As if I cared.

"He says too much freedom is bad for people. Most people don't even want to be free. Not totally free. We just *think* we do. If anybody ever gave us total freedom, we'd give it right back to him and say, 'Here, take it. I don't want it. I can't handle it.'"

"So?" I said.

He chuckled. "So" — he tore a piece off my licorice — "just seeing you there made me think about that. Guess I'm going batty, huh?"

"Guess so," I agreed.

He left. I called. "Hey, Ham."

"What?" He stayed in the hallway, out of sight.

"How come you're not hollering at me about your ice cream anymore?"

"Why should I? You never take it, right?"

"I know. But you used to holler anyway."

His head swung into my doorway. Grinning. "Maybe my throat's sore."

I smelled a rat.

Next day Ham was out in the yard, playing with his vegetables and dried cow poop. He planted tomatoes, peppers, and eggplants. None of them amount to anything yet. The tomatoes are just some puny yellow blossoms and a couple tiny green nubs. But whenever he sees something new he goes screaming into the house and drags my mother out to see. He's convinced we're going to be eating our own vegetables all winter long because of three bags of dried cow poop.

Anyway, I made the mistake of being in the yard at the same time as him. And sure enough, he looks up from a tomato stalk and says, " 'Bout ready to mow that grass, ol' boy?"

In less than two seconds I was on my bike, my glove swinging on the handlebars. That's when I finally shoved off into summer.

We got our baseball games going at the park. Dugan (you could tell it was officially summer because he had his tie off), who never brings anything of his own — ball, bat, or glove — showed up this year with a ball. A brand-new one. We all crowded around it, gawking at it in his hand.

"Man!" I said. "Look at it!"

"It's white as a bone," said Calvin.

Peter said, "Look at the writing on it. I didn't know they had writing on them."

"Sure they do," I told him. "When they're new."

"Can I hold it?" Richie said.

"Where'd you get it?" I said.

Dugan handed it to Richie. "I found it."

Which was probably true. Things happen to Dugan that

don't happen to regular people. Like, Dugan is always just *showing up*, right? Well, it sort of works the other way too: things are always showing up *on* Dugan. Money. Food. Bicycles. Now a new baseball.

I don't mean he steals. Things just come to him. Like at the baseball games, he uses our gloves and bats. His bicycles are jalopies. None of the rest of us would ever touch the things he rides. But you got to give him credit: he gets them for nothing. He sees one that somebody's throwing out in the trash — he'll take it. Even if it's only got one pedal, or the wheel's bent, or it's a girl's. He gets three or four a year that way.

As usual, Ham had his own weird and half-funny way of putting it: "Your friend Dugan just rolls down the hill of life, and when he reaches the bottom he gets up and picks from his clothes and pockets everything that stuck to him on the way down."

I took the baseball off Richie. It was beautiful, all right. You could see every little red stitch. There wasn't a single nick in the hide. Perfectly smooth. Gleaming white. I put it to my nose. It was so new it hardly had a smell.

"Why don't we keep it like this for a while," I said. "For something important." I had a black-tape ball with me.

"Just for lookin' at," said Calvin.

Dugan nodded. He held his hand out. I gave him the ball, and before anybody could stop him, he wound up and fired it with all his might. It went skipping and scraping along the infield, smacked off the side of a dugout, and rolled into the trees toward the creek. We took off after it. We found it in the muddy rocks. It wasn't a new ball, not anymore. Dugan was still there grinning when we carried it back.

I had a pretty good day at the plate: seven singles, fourteen doubles, five triples, and eleven homeruns. Pretty good day in the field too: only two errors. I missed a couple other grounders, but they were bad hops. It's not my fault if the field is full of stones.

But I didn't have a pretty good day at the nose or the raccoon.

This was the day I started one of my summer projects: to learn to blow my nose like Ricky Mains. Ricky Mains was a great shortstop last year for the Avon Oaks High School team. He played in the America Legion all-star game in the city, and he was signed up by the Milwaukee Brewers. He's playing on their AA minor league team right now. Well, I saw him do it once at a Legion game. He pressed the side of one nostril with his fingertip — like pressing a button — then he blew, and — *pow!* — out the other nostril it shot to the ground. Like a bullet. Must have left a regular crater in the dust. Then he switched nostrils.

Of course, I realize a lot of people do it that way. Especially athletes and lifeguards. I almost got hit walking under a lifeguard stand once. I think the best I ever saw at it was a marathon runner. He was coming down a hill blowing to the left and right without losing a stride. But I want to pattern myself after Ricky Mains as much as I can. I figure if you want to be a major league shortstop, you better learn to blow your nose like one. Someday maybe there'll be a scouting report on me: "Hits: Fair. Fields: Great. Blows Nose: Can't-miss prospect."

So the time came. I was in the field, out at shortstop, nobody paying any attention to me. Just to warm up, to get the feel of it, I pressed my nostril and tried a few little *fhnns.*

Nothing. I could tell right away there was no half-ass way to do this. I pressed. I blew. Nothing but air. I closed my eyes, tried harder. Nothing — except a sharp pain that shot up to my eye and into my brain.

I saw what the problem was: I wasn't loaded up enough. So for the next hour or so I forced myself not to sniff once. It's not easy, especially when you can feel the little buggers creeping down your nose. Not only that, but I had a truck-load of dust from the field coming in the other way.

When I could hardly breathe anymore, I figured I was ready for another try. I spread my feet, leaned forward a little, pressed, closed my eyes, blew: *FHNNNN!*

Eewww.

Something came out, all right. But it wasn't neat and sharp as a bullet, and it never did reach the ground. I took my shirt off and cleaned myself with it.

Well, Ricky Mains probably didn't do it right the first time either. Practice makes perfect. I wasn't going to give up. But I *was* going to start carrying a handkerchief for a backup.

As for the raccoon, we saw it late in the afternoon, when it was almost time to quit and go home for dinner. It was out in left field, sort of moseying along toward centerfield.

Dugan spied it first. He let out a yell — "Raccoon!" — and tore off after it with a bat and ball. We all followed, scooping up stones and anything else along the way.

The raccoon saw us and took off. He was heading for the drainpipe in center. We tried to cut him off. Ahead of us Dugan winged the ball, but it missed by ten feet. Then he dug in, leaned back like a grenade thrower, and slung the bat. It cartwheeled through the air and bounced down just behind the raccoon.

Meanwhile, the rest of us are war-whooping and moose-calling and sending out a barrage of stones, rocks, bottles, tree limbs, baseball gloves, and chewed-up bubblegum. None of us hit it. We were pretty close by the time the raccoon reached the drainpipe. We got there just after it ducked inside.

I had a soda bottle left. Everybody else was out of ammo. "Geteem, Herk!" Dugan was screaming. I ran up alongside the pipe and whipped the bottle into the dark, round hole. It never broke. You could hear it rattling along the pipe. But before the rattle there was another sound — a kind of soft thud.

I turned back. All of a sudden I didn't feel so good. Dugan was screaming in my ear, "You goteem! You goteem!" The others, the smiles on their faces were different. They were looking everyplace but at me.

Dugan goes, "Anybody got a flashlight?" He doesn't even wait for the answer. He gets down on his hands and knees and puts his face right into the mouth of the pipe, trying to see.

The whistle blew at the bubblegum factory. "It's five o'clock," Peter said. "I gotta go."

"Me too," said Calvin.

Four of us headed back across the field to our bikes. Dugan was a madman at the pipe. "Who gotta match? Who gotta match?" he kept going. He was grabbing dry weeds and sticks and making a little pile on the lip of the pipe. He kept calling us all the way across the field: "Let's smokeem out! Let's smokeem out!"

I kept looking back, wondering if the raccoon was dead. This was the second time in one year I hit something I never thought I would. When would I learn my lesson?

I pedaled home. I prayed Dugan wouldn't find a match.

The next day was pretty much Calvin's. He knows I'm interested in science and all, so he asked me over.

I couldn't believe his room. It looks like Frankenstein's laboratory. With a bed. The first thing you notice is this skeleton hanging from the ceiling. Only it's not a whole skeleton. It only has one leg, half its ribs, no hands, and no head. It's not real either. It's from a kit Calvin sent away for. The bones are made of some kind of plastic or cement or something. Calvin is making the thing one bone at a time. On each bone he writes its name with a black felt-tip pen.

No posters of rock or TV stars on Calvin's walls. He's got these two charts as big as window shades showing the human body. One male and one female. I found out a lot of stuff I didn't know. For instance, fallopian tubes aren't where I thought they were. And they're a lot smaller.

Then there were all the dead things. I don't just mean seventeen-year locust shells (which I collect myself) or a neat butterfly or two. I mean he's got a million bottles and jars filled with alcohol on his dresser and bookcase, and every one has something in it.

I jumped back when I saw one of them. "What's that?" I almost yelled. It looked like a black, fat mouse.

"A mole," he said. "Look at the feet. And the nose."

He was right. The feet were like paddles with little claws sticking out. And the nose was long and snouty and funny-looking.

"And look," he said. "No eyes."

"Don't they see?" I asked him.

"Nah. They don't have to. They're blind. They just go underground."

"So how'd you get it?"

"I just found it down the street one day. I don't know why it came up." He put the jar up to the light and turned it around. The mole bobbed a little in the alcohol.

I thought to myself, there's something inside out about a kid that hates chili but keeps a dead mole in his bedroom.

In another jar he had the humongousest beetle I ever saw. Green. In perfect shape. Like it was made of plastic.

Naturally he has all kinds of other bugs too. I recognized some of them, but *some* of them — man! — there's enough there for the Japanese movie directors to start a whole new series of monster flicks. And Calvin says he got every one of them without going outside Avon Oaks.

Besides bugs and the mole, some of the other things he has in jars are garter snakes, salamanders, crawfish, minnows, two birds, worms, caterpillars, a mouse, a tadpole, a toad, and a box turtle.

Most of them he found already dead, he said. If he had to kill any, it would only be in the cause of science and research. And even for science and research, he had to let me know, he would never kill anything with hair, feathers, or fur. (Like a raccoon, for instance.)

"What's all this got to do with medicine, anyway?" I asked him. "I thought you wanted to be a doctor."

"It's all life," he goes. "Life is life. I don't know what I'm gonna specialize in yet. I can learn a lot studying these things. Doncha know we got a lot in common with bugs and birds and all?"

I told him just having to share Avon Oaks with some of those bugs was enough to have in common for me.

Then he took me to the kitchen and opened up the freezer and took out a macaroni-salad container and took off the lid and showed me the inside. It wasn't macaroni salad. There were three things. They looked exactly like worms.

They were.

"Cryogenics," he goes. He took one out and held it up by one end. It's hard to explain the feeling you get watching a worm stand straight up between somebody's fingertips. "I froze 'em. Now I'm gonna see if I can bring 'em back."

"Fantastic!" I said. And I told him about the Freeze-Dried Grandmother Launch Pad I made for Peter Kim. He said great, we could collaborate. We could start out on worms and someday work our way up to grandmothers. Win the Nobel Prize. We agreed it's amazing how great minds run in the same track.

He kept the worm he was holding and put the other two back in the freezer. He put the worm on a paper towel. "I put them in a week ago," he said. "I'm gonna take one out each week. This one's the first."

We sat at the kitchen table watching the frozen worm. It was like you see on TV when somebody's in a coma: you're afraid to take your eyes away so you don't miss some slight movement. Calvin especially. He was like a hawk over that worm. He kept rolling it over with a toothpick. He poked it a little here and poked it there.

We waited a whole hour for that sucker and all it did was thaw out. You could see the toothpick making bigger and bigger dents in it.

"How long we gonna wait?" I said.

Calvin looked up at the clock. "That's it," he goes. "It ain't comin' back."

It only took him five seconds to spear the worm with the toothpick, carry it to the back door, and flip it outside.

I was surprised at how fast and easy he did it. How he could be so interested in the worm one minute, then throw it right out without batting an eye. I said so.

"That's research," he goes. "The scientific method. We might have to try a million worms before we succeed. Besides, I'm practicing."

"Practicing what?" I said.

"Not getting too involved with your patients. Half of them go dying on ya. You can't afford to like them too much, y'know? You'd go crazy, I read." He snapped the toothpick and threw it into the wastebasket. "You gotta be hard to be a doctor."

Then he told me about his next experiment. It had to do with lightning bugs. He wanted to perform a transplant. Transplant a lightning bug's flasher onto some other kind of bug.

I asked him what for.

He shrugged. "I don't know."

That didn't sound like Calvin. I told him he wasn't being very scientific.

He looks up at the ceiling and gives this smug little grin. "Ever hear of pure research?"

"*Pure* research?"

"Yeah. Pure."

"No," I said. "That supposed to be different from other kinds of research?"

"Yep," he goes. "Pure research is the best kind of research

of all. It's when you do something just to find out what'll happen. Not so you can make a million dollars off it."

"So what *do* you do it for?" I asked the grand wizard.

He sniffed at the ceiling. "Knowledge. Maybe a thousand years later somebody'll come along and make something out of what you discover. But as far as you're concerned, all you want to do is add a little bit to the knowledge of mankind." He leaned back on the hind legs of his chair. "That's *pure* research."

He leaned back too far, and he and the chair went crashing to the floor. What came out of my mouth was *pure* laughter.

So much for the first two working days of vacation. Little by little I settled into my summer schedule.

1. I rode my bike. I rode past Debbie Breen's house a lot.
2. I played ball at the park. I kept track of my hitting. After two weeks I was batting .920 and I had forty-one homeruns. I was aiming for last summer's record of three hundred nineteen homers. I still wasn't having much success with the Ricky Mains nose-blow though.
3. I kept an eye on the drainpipe in centerfield.
4. I taught the corner kids. They started to figure I know a lot more than just making paper airplanes. They stopped waiting for me to get to them. As soon as they spotted me riding down the street they came running and yelling: Jason! Jason! C'mere! Jason, look. Jason, how do you do this? Jason, what about that? Every day they had a new question or a new problem waiting

for me to solve. I passed a lot of good stuff onto them. I showed them how to pour salt on a snail. How to make Popsicle-stick things. How to leave a piece of candy in the middle of the sidewalk to attract a million ants and gross out the grownups passing by. How to take care of a scab. How to tell poison ivy. How to act if a bee comes around. How to find neat stuff at the sewer grates after storms. How to clean out your bellybutton lint.

When I tried to tell them about *Pioneer,* though, they didn't understand. They're not old enough yet to be amazed at distances like that.

5. When I got desperate for money, I grabbed Richie and we bagged groceries for a day.

6. Mostly I was outside. I pretty much let my space station slide. When I did come inside during the day, it was usually to check the refrigerator. All that heat and sweat calls for a lot of ice cream. But, starting one day, I had to settle for cold water. There wasn't a spoonful of ice cream in the freezer.

I couldn't understand it. I knew our half-gallon was gone, but there was always a box of Ham's Dutch chocolate almond in there. Then I went upstairs and looked in Ham's study, and I knew why he stopped hollering about his ice cream disappearing. There on the floor next to a bookcase was this little white baby freezer — with a padlock on it.

LITTLE BROTHERS

RICHIE'S PARENTS GOT A TENT. A BIG ONE. THEY'RE GOING camping later this summer.

Richie asked if he could bring it over to my yard — he only lives across the street — so we could give it a test run. His parents said okay.

Dugan wasn't around. Calvin was doing his lightning-bug transplant that night. So that left three of us: me, Richie, and Peter Kim.

We weren't allowed to bring the tent over and set it up until after dinner, so we all just hung around my yard and talked about it and figured where it would go and made plans for the night and just in general got all excited.

We were sitting on the back steps drinking ice tea and discussing things when I thought I saw something under the snowball bush. I went over for a look. It was my brontosaurus.

I howled. "Timmy!"

My mother opened the screen door. "What now?"

"Look!" I hollered. "I got him his own for Christmas, and he *still* takes mine!"

As usual she takes his side. "He has good taste. He knows yours are better."

I shoved it at her. "Look!"

"What's the matter with it?"

"It's all muddy and messed up!"

"Can't you clean it?"

"I shouldn't *have* to clean it! He shouldn't be touching it!" I screamed my lungs out. "IT'S MINE!"

Richie and Peter got down from the steps and sort of backed away. My mother was staying calm and patient. She just blinked and gawked at me for a while. She couldn't believe how mad I was. A fly went in right past her, but she kept the door open.

I looked down at my dinosaur. I always kept it so clean. I was sick. I ground my teeth. "That's the last time."

"Jason," she goes, soft.

"He's not gettin' another chance."

Her voice snapped sharp this time. "Jason."

"The. Last. Time."

The door slammed behind her. "Jason!"

"What?"

"Now you stop that. You do *not* talk like that. Timmy is your little brother. You want to know something? You're nicer to those little boys on the corner than you are to your own brother. Did you know that?"

I wanted to say, Yeah, I know. I know it's a crime when I throw your ratty old crown, but it's okay for him to ruin my dinosaur. I said, "No."

She softened up. Smiled. "He's little. Timmy's little. You know why he takes your dinosaurs? Jason?"

"Yeah. He's a thief."

"He takes them because you're his big brother."

"Great," I said. "Where do I resign?"

"He takes them because he looks up to you. You're special to him."

"Great."

"Your things seem special to him. *Because* they're yours. See? That's why he likes to play with your things: just because they *are* yours. If they weren't yours"— she chuckled — "he wouldn't even want them."

"Great," I said, and walked away.

I just walked around the yard for a while, stewing in the sun. I had the brontosaurus by the neck, like a club.

Peter and Richie joined me. Little by little we got back to talking about camping out. But Peter seemed a little different, not so interested anymore. Sure enough, after a while he says, "Uh, you guys . . . I don't think I'll be coming over tonight."

We asked him why not.

He scrunched up his face. "Well . . . I forgot to tell you. My mother wanted Kippy to come along tonight too."

Oh shit, I thought. Which is what I could tell Richie thought too. But we never let it show to Peter. So I just said, "Well, it's okay with me. But he's kinda young, ain't he?"

"She said she's not afraid as long as she knows we're all at your place. She said Kippy likes you."

I was shocked. "Me?"

He shrugged. "That's what she says. He talks about you sometimes." He looked at Richie. "You too."

"So?" I said. "What's the problem? Why can'tcha come?"

He picked up a leaf and started folding it, real neat. "Well . . . I know you don't want little kids around. He'd spoil it all."

You can say that again, I thought. "Look," I said. "For you to come, does he have to come too?"

"Besides," he said, "I think my mother thought Timmy was gonna be there too."

"Peter," I said, "you're avoiding the question. Does he have to come if you come?"

He looked away and nodded. "Yep."

"Okay," I said. "So that's it. You're comin'."

"Nah," he goes.

I grab him by the arm and look him in the eye. "Peter, listen. I said you're coming. I don't mind having Kippy around. I just thought maybe he was a little too young to go sleeping out. That's all. Okay?"

He wagged his head. "I don't know. He'll spoil things."

"Spoil things? Waddaya mean?" I sort of ranted like a courtroom lawyer. "Spoil things? For who? He's not gonna spoil anything for me. Richie, he gonna spoil anything for you?"

Richie goes, "Nope."

"See?" I said. "That just leaves you. *You're* the one that don't want him to come. You bum. You hate your little brother."

Peter couldn't help laughing. He left and said they'd be back after dinner.

"Great," I groaned when Peter was gone. "Just great. Here we're all ready to camp out and we gotta take that little fart with us." I looked at my brontosaurus, which I was still grabbing by the neck. "Man. This is sure turning out to be a great damn day, ain't it?"

We got another ice tea and spent the rest of the afternoon grumping and bitching about our bad luck. It was even worse for me than Richie, because I had the two things to complain about: Kippy coming over, plus my dinosaur. I kept switching back and forth. I couldn't decide which one made me madder.

Then, just before dinner, the two came into my head at the same time and kind of oozed and mixed together, until all of a sudden they weren't two separate complaints anymore, but one new idea.

I told Richie about it. He loved it. "Kinda like what they did to you at the hayride," he said. "With the dragon."

That didn't occur to me. "Yeah," I said. "Kinda. And the thing is, we kill two birds with one stone. We teach Timmy a lesson about taking my dinosaurs, and maybe Kippy'll get scared enough so he won't *want* to keep coming around with us anymore."

"Yeah," Richie said.

"Yeah," I said.

Richie ran home for dinner.

My problem now was to get Timmy to come along camping with us. After what I said to my mother about him, I couldn't exactly tell her I'd love to have him join us. So what I did was, I worked it through him. I passed him on the stairs and whispered, "We're camping out in the yard tonight and you're not." I knew he would take it from there.

All dinner long he bugged my mom and Ham to let him camp outside with us. My mother kept telling him he was too little, all the time giving me these dirty looks. I just ate.

Then after dinner I whispered to him in the living room, "Little Kippy's coming too."

Into the kitchen he goes bawling. "Mom-meee! Little Kippy's coming too!"

I just kind of hung around. I knew sooner or later my

mother would want me. In the meantime I just let Timmy do the work.

Finally my mother came out of the kitchen. She kind of plants herself and glares at me for a minute. There's a dishrag in her hand. "Jason, are you going to let him camp with you tonight?"

I had to be careful not to look too anxious. "I don't know," I said. "It's not my tent."

"It's your yard."

"It's *your* yard."

"*Is* Kippy Kim coming along tonight with Peter?"

"I guess."

"Well, is he?"

"Peter said he is."

"Well then," she said, "I think Timmy should be allowed to go too."

She was waiting for my answer.

I shrugged.

"Okay, Timmy," she said, heading back to the kitchen. "You're going."

Timmy goes, "Ya-hoo!"

Yeah, I grin to myself, *ya-hoo*.

There's a round, bare patch of ground in the back of our yard. It's where Timmy had a little plastic wading pool last summer. We put up the tent right alongside the bare patch.

The tent was plenty big, and it was really neat inside. It had its own canvas floor and mosquito net at the doorway and all. Richie was the only one with a real sleeping bag. The rest of us made up our own with blankets and sheets and stuff.

Just as I expected, the little kids were a pain. They kept

screaming with delight at every little thing, like they were never outside their house before. You would have thought lightning bugs were made of candy, the way they went crazy over them. (*God help some poor lightning bug over in Calvin's yard*, I thought.)

They kept nagging us to play their little kiddie games. They jumped on our backs while we were trying to talk, and the more we shook them off the more they came jumping back. Once I felt wet on the back of my neck. Kippy peed himself. If Peter wasn't there I would have killed him.

Even I was surprised at how bad they were. You'd think they would appreciate being allowed to be with us, and keep their mouths shut and be half good. But no. They had to bug us and climb all over us and tick us off. "Okay," I kept warning them, "Okay-ay."

After a while I couldn't even stand the sight of Kippy's Phillies cap.

When it got completely dark we all had to stay in the tent. Richie had a lantern. He lit it. My mother brought out some french fries she made in the oven. And some catsup and salt and some Hawaiian Punch.

After a while Richie's eyes shot open and he goes, "Eeeww, God!"

I knew before I turned to look exactly what it was, because it always happens when you put Timmy and french fries together in the absence of parents. Sure enough, there was Timmy, this big silly grin on his face, sticking the soles of his bare feet out at us, and between each pair of toes was a french fry.

Naturally Kippy had to do it too, and they both thought that was the funniest thing since mud. Pretty soon Richie and Peter are laughing too. They couldn't help it. I almost couldn't help it myself. But whenever I felt a laugh ready to pop out, I took a good look at my brontosaurus, which I brought along with me, and I wouldn't feel like laughing anymore.

I waited till it got pretty late. Us big kids played a game of Monopoly. Then we switched to cards. The little kids were playing with their little green soldiers. I said I had to go to the bathroom and left.

Actually I just went around to the bare patch. The flashlight and Ham's garden trowel were waiting where I left them. I turned the flashlight onto the bare patch, grabbed the trowel, and started digging.

I could have gone faster, but I had to be quiet so the little kids wouldn't hear. I dug deep — about six inches — and by the time I was through I used up just about the whole patch. I pushed away the dug-up dirt and made the shape of the hole as clear and sharp as possible, so anybody, even a little kid, taking a look at it could tell right away exactly what it was: a dinosaur footprint.

I stepped back. It was a masterpiece. And a big sucker, all right. Almost scared me. I had to keep shining the flashlight back and forth before it finally covered the whole thing. I stood in the middle of it. Five or six more of me could have stood there too.

I went over near the kitchen door, cupped my hands, and let out a good dinosaur roar. Then I went back to the tent.

The little kids were at the front flap, wanting to look out, but afraid.

"Hey, you guys," I said, acting all excited. "You oughta see what's on the news on TV!"

Richie said, "What, Jason?"

Peter had a little grin in his eye. We told him we were

going to play a little joke on the kids, but we didn't tell him exactly what. The three of us pretended just to be with ourselves, but we were all watching the little kids out of the corner of our eyes.

I go, "A dinosaur! They were digging coal up north and they came to this humongous cave and at the end of the cave there was this big jungle and all of a sudden this dinosaur comes charging out at them!"

"Man!" said Richie.

"Wow!" said Peter.

By now the little kids were standing right behind me.

"Yeah," I go, "and the dinosaur ran through the mining town and stomped on all the mine shafts! So there's a thousand miners trapped down below now!"

"Man!"

"Wow!"

"And then the dinosaur saw a train goin' by, and he picked it up and threw it in the river!"

Richie said, "How big is he?"

"Big as our house," I said.

Everybody looked at the tent wall in the direction of our house.

"Wow," said Peter.

"Know Phoenixville?" I said.

Timmy spoke up behind me. "Yeah. I know it."

"It ate half the people in Phoenixville."

Kippy squeaked, "It like people?"

"I guess so," I said. "Must've been hungry. Ever hear of Littleton Lake Park?"

"Yeah," says Timmy.

"It got thirsty and drank Littleton Lake and all the people swimming in it."

The three of us had to turn away so the little kids wouldn't see us cracking up. When I could talk straight again, I said, "And y'know where they said it's heading for?"

Timmy and Kippy are both gawking up at me, their eyes and their mouths wide open. Finally Timmy says, his voice all raspy, "No."

"Avon Oaks," I said.

I couldn't stand it looking at their faces. Especially Kippy's in that Phillies cap. I kept my eyes aimed at Richie and Peter. "Yeah," I said, "they lost track of it in the dark. They don't know where it is exactly. Except it was last seen heading for Avon Oaks." I winked at Richie. "They said it roars."

"Hey," Richie goes, "like this?" He gives a roar. A pretty dinky roar.

"Nah," I said. "Like this." And I do one just like before. The little kids are down there grabbing at our legs.

"Yeah!" goes Richie. "That's it!"

"That's what?" I say.

"Know when you went out to go to the bathroom?"

"Yeah."

"Know when you were coming back?"

"Yeah."

"Well, just before you came back, we heard a sound like that." He looked down at the little kids. "Didn't we?"

They were just a pair of open mouths now. They both nodded.

"See?" said Richie. "We all heard it."

"Well," I said, "what do you think it means?"

The three of us kind of looked from one to the other. For some strange reason, none of us wanted to be the one that came right out and said it. Then, up comes Timmy's voice: "The dinosaur's here."

I swear, the way he said it, I almost believed it myself.

I said, "Nah. There ain't no dinosaur out there. I was just out there. There's nothin' to be scared of."

"Then go ahead out again," Richie says.

"Okay. Gimme the lantern."

I grabbed the lantern and went out and walked around the yard, pretending to look for a dinosaur. They were all watching from the flap.

On the way back I called, "See? Toldja. Nothing to be scared of. Nothin' here but lightning bugs." Then, as I walked into the bare patch, I pretended to trip and fall.

Richie called out, "what happened?"

I groaned, "I fell in a hole."

"You okay?"

"I sprained my ankle." I gave a good grunt. "I can't get up. I need some help."

When they came out Richie pretended to help me up. "Man!" I said. "That was a big hole. I didn't know we had a hole there."

"You didn't," said Richie. "You didn't have a hole there. I know your yard good as my own. There was never no hole there."

"Well, there is now," I said. And as I said it I swung the lantern out real slow over the patch. The lantern light was bigger than the flashlight light, and it covered the whole patch.

"That ain't no hole," Richie says.

"Peter," I say, "what's it look like?"

Peter pretended to study it. "Looks like a footprint to me."

"An animal footprint," I said.

"A bi-i-ig animal," goes Richie.

I gulped. "My God! It's the dinosaur!"

Kippy squeals, "Pee-er."

"You goin' in now?" Timmy looks up at me.

I pretend to think. "Nah, guess not. I better stay out here."

"Okay," Timmy goes.

"Okay what?"

"I'm stayin' too."

"Pee-er," Kippy squeals.

I pounded my fist into my palm. "Dinosaur or no dinosaur," I growled, "I'm stayin'."

"Me too," goes Timmy.

"I don't care *how* big he is."

"Me too."

"I don't care *how* many people he ate."

"Me too."

"I don't care if he's right there on the other side of the house, even."

Timmy gets behind me. "Me too."

That's enough for Kippy. He really starts up. He's wailing away: "Pee-er! Pee-er! Yet's go! I'm cared! Yet's go home! Yet's go home!"

We tried to quiet him down, but he just got worse. He kept looking at the footprint and yelling and pulling on Peter. He pulled him out to the middle of the yard. I could hear Peter trying to tell him it was just a joke, but Kippy wouldn't listen. He was hysterical: "Yet's go home! Yet's go home!"

Peter didn't have a choice. He had to take him home. By this time Ham and my mom were at the window of my room, wanting to know what was going on. We said Peter and Kippy had to go. My mother said they couldn't walk home alone this late. Somebody would have to drive them. Ham drove them.

When they left, my mother tried to weasel out of Timmy what happened. He tried not to tell, but then he caved in. She blew her stack. She made him go in. She said the only reason she was letting me stay out was because of Richie.

By now she was down at the back door. Her favorite place to holler at me from. I tried to tell her it was just a joke. I was just giving Timmy a little lesson so he wouldn't take my dinosaurs anymore, I explained.

"I'll be the one to give any lessons around here," she goes. "You're not his judge and jury."

"Well, you never do anything to him," I told her. "I wanted him to stop stealing my dinosaurs, so I did something about it. He could smash every one of my dinosaurs and nobody would do a thing."

She wagged her finger at me. "You just take care of yourself, buster. I'll take care of him."

I hate being called buster. I said out loud what I only thought before. "Yeah. He can ruin my dinosaurs and nothing ever happens to him, but if I throw some old crown across a room I'm the worst criminal there ever was."

"Enjoy yourself tonight," she said. "You won't be going out after dinner for a week."

"What!"

"And keep your voice down. You're getting too smart, boy. Maybe you should've been suspended for more than one day. You're getting too much mouth."

The door slammed shut.

Back in the tent, Richie shut up while I fumed and cursed. We laid down, and I was *still* fuming. Then, when I finally ran out of gas, he says, "Glad I don't have a little brother."

"You oughta be," I told him. "They ruin your whole damn life."

Richie turned out the lantern. "Night," he said.

"Night," I said.

I thought about how true it was, what I said about little brothers. Because they're little they get excused for everything. They don't stick to their own kind. They don't know when they're not wanted. You can't get rid of them. It's impossible. You can't even escape from them. They take your stuff. And what's worse, they treat it like it's theirs. The only way you can keep your stuff away from them is to lock it up twenty-four hours a day — and then *you* couldn't use it. They'll leave your baseball glove out in the rain. And to top it all off, you can't even play a trick on them. The whole thing winds up backfiring and all you get is yourself grounded for a week.

"Your whole damn life," I whispered into the dark.

In the yard, on the other side of the mosquito netting, the lightning bugs were blinking away like nothing in the world was wrong.

During dinner the next night the phone rang. My mother answered it. She listened for a couple seconds, then she gasped. Her eyes bulged. "How?" she said. She listened some more, then hung up. She stared around the table at each of us, with glassy eyes. She couldn't seem to find the right one to stare at.

"Kippy Kim was just killed in a car accident," she said.

HEADLIGHTS

WE WALKED TO THE FUNERAL HOME FOR THE VIEWING. I picked up Richie. Then the two of us picked up Calvin. It seemed funny not picking up Peter too. Dugan didn't show up.

The parking lot was full.

We got scared at first — the people coming out and hanging around the door, crying.

A man in a suit said, "Good evening. Kim or Miraglia?"

I didn't understand. "Herkimer," I said. "Jason."

He seemed confused. He looked at a piece of paper. Looked at us. "Are you boys here to see Philip Kim?"

"No," I said.

Calvin jabbed me. "Yes we are. That's his real name."

The man turned sideways and held out his arm. "To the right, boys."

The place was mobbed. Where there weren't people there were flowers. It looked like Hawaii.

We kind of hung back for a while. Looking. We all knew exactly where Kippy was — up there in the middle of all the flowers — but I guess we wanted to think this was just another room.

Most of the people I never saw before. There were a couple teachers I recognized from grade school, even though Kippy didn't start kindergarten yet. My mother was up at the front, kneeling, talking to Mrs. Kim.

We could only see Peter's back. He was standing at the coffin. He didn't move, just looked down. Other people kept filing up and looking and praying and moving away. But Peter just stayed there. Some of them touched his shoulder when they passed. He didn't seem to notice.

Some of the people crossed themselves. They were Catholics.

I whispered to Calvin, "What are they?"

"Who?"

"The Kims."

"You mean Korean or American?"

"Their religion."

Calvin didn't know. Neither did Richie. But a grownup right in back of us leaned down and whispered, "Presbyterian."

We hung back as long as we could. First one of us would say, "You ready?" Then another would say it. But all three of us were never ready at the same time.

But finally we had to. We waited till there was no line, then we went.

It was like being on stage. Everybody looking at us looking at Kippy. If I didn't know any better, I wouldn't have thought anything was wrong with him, except he had a suit on. Even his Phillies cap was there. And some toys. He looked like he was sleeping.

"Hi, Peter," I said.

He opened his mouth but nothing came out. Teardrop streaks were on his cheeks.

"You okay?" I said.

He nodded.

We just stood there. Some more people were lining up. "Well . . . be seein' ya," I said.

He nodded. He never took his eyes off the coffin.

When we got to the back again I saw Calvin wasn't with us. He was just then leaving the coffin. He came at us crying and not even trying to hide it. I guess being hardhearted about worms wasn't very good practice in getting ready for Kippy Kim. I decided not to ask him how the lightning bug transplant turned out.

We went back out. The man at the door said, "Goodnight, boys."

It was dark out. The moon looked like a brand-new baseball hanging over the parking lot.

On the way home we didn't look at each other. Or talk.

We rode with our parents the next day to the church. When we came out to go to the cemetery, there was a sticker on our windshield saying "FUNERAL." A man poked his head in and said, "Lights."

We went real slow. We went through red lights, stop signs — nothing could stop us. I looked up ahead and back; I couldn't believe how long the line of cars was.

At the grave we stuck with our families. They gave us flowers to put on the coffin. The Kims were still there when we walked away.

It was a big cemetery. Rolling hills. On the farthest hill somebody was standing. It was Dugan.

THE DARK

I NEVER THOUGHT THAT MUCH ABOUT THE DARK BEFORE. NOW I don't like it.

At first I left the light on, and when my mother asked why, I told her I fell asleep reading.

Then I rigged up my space station with lights. Little train-type lights. Red. Green. Yellow. Blue. My favorite is a big white one that blinks. I lay there looking at the little dots of light in the dark.

I work on my space station a lot. I keep making improvements. It's going to have everything. It won't need Earth at all. The kids will still go to school, but it won't be like here. There won't be any tests, and you can take any subject you want. For instance, if you want to take a course in bike riding, or making paper airplanes, you can. The other main difference is, there won't be any ninth-graders.

I stopped keeping track of my hitting at the park. Sometimes we let a stray kid in. But most of the time it's only three or four of us. Now that Peter isn't out in centerfield anymore, we all have to do a lot more running and chasing after balls. For the first time in my life I play other positions than shortstop. I never knew what the world looked like from the outfield.

I don't like the outfield. You have to run so far after balls. You're all alone. It's so quiet out there, just you and the ball. You can hear your feet running. They seem to say, *Kippy's dead. Kippy's dead. Kippy's dead.*

Every time I go up to bat I look at the drainpipe out in centerfield. I don't know why, but I get more and more anxious to see that raccoon come out of that hole. I keep looking and it keeps not coming out.

I ride my bike a lot. I don't ride past the corner kids anymore. I go another way. There's things I ought to be telling them, and I want to tell them, but I just sort of can't.

Sometimes, even with the space station lights, I still can't sleep, so I go downstairs and onto the porch. The first time I did it I couldn't believe how different things are at three o'clock in the morning. My first thought was: *Jeez! They change planets on you at night!*

Once, riding my bike, I saw a dead crow in the street. I stopped and looked. Cars were going by. Each time a car tire whizzed real close, even though most of the crow was mashed into the street, the end of one wing would kind of flutter in the air.

It's been really hot out. Everything is snaily.

I see old ladies grinning. Especially in the supermarkets. And on Sundays. After a while it got to me. I tried scowling at one right in her face, just to see what would happen. She just kept grinning away. Someday I'm going to find out what they're all grinning about.

One night it rained. Then stopped. I listened at the

window. The whole night was crackling and popping, like everything was ready to come to a boil. No wonder. Baseball ... Kippy Kim in a coffin ... sunshine ... dead crows ... Debbie Breen ... grinning old hags ... bugs ... bicycles ... bellybutton lint — God! How can such different kind of stuff all fit in the same world? Much less the same thirteen-year-old head?

I dream about *Pioneer*. Sailing out toward Pluto. The golden man and lady tumbling out of the Solar System. Sometimes I wish it would turn back. Sometimes I dream it does. It's right outside my window, bobbing like a buoy, waiting for me to add something to it — my little gift to worldkind — to take out to the stars. I squirm and sweat and get panicky, because I don't know what to contribute, and *Pioneer* can't wait any longer.

GIRL

I WAS OUT RIDING MY BIKE. NOTHING ELSE TO DO. HOW LONG can you stand to hang around your house? Even my space station was getting a little boring. Baseball? Forget it. Calvin was away at the beach. Richie away at the mountains. Peter — just — away. And Dugan doesn't show up unless there's at least two people.

So I decided to ride — far. I filled my canteen with water and strapped it on my bike and got an advance on my allowance to buy something at a McDonald's.

First I swung by the park to check out the drainpipe: no raccoon. Then I headed out of town. Past the state hospital. Past the community college. I turned down a road I was never on before, and pretty soon there were no sidewalks or traffic lights. Then the gutters and drainpipes went, and most of the houses. Lots of trees though. The road got crunchier and skinny and curvy. Sometimes when a car came along I got squeezed over and whipped in the legs by stems and thorns hanging out.

Then the farms started. Fields, corn, cows, silos, fences:

farm stuff. It wasn't even noon yet, but already the road ahead was starting to shimmer, that's how hot it was. Every once in a while I stopped to take a small swig from my canteen. I kept my eye out for a McDonald's.

Most of the going was up and down hills, but it was on a rare level stretch where I spotted something far ahead, oozing in and out of the heat-shimmer. A bike! It disappeared around a bend. I stepped on it, and when I spotted it again it was clear of the shimmer. Sky blue bike . . . red butt on black seat . . . red shorts . . . floppy red hat . . . bare feet . . . *girl*.

I slowed down, wasn't sure I wanted to make contact, thought about turning around, didn't want to do that either. Then suddenly she stopped. She was reaching into a clump of bushes. She heard me coming, looked up. It was Call-Me-Marceline McAllister.

I don't know why, I couldn't explain it in a million years, but I was glad — I think. I pulled up.

"You?" she said. I wasn't sure if her tone meant disapproval or surprise.

"Who else?" I answered. I was cool.

She went back to reaching in the bush. "I wouldn't expect to see you out here."

"Why not?" I said. "I ride my bike all over." She didn't answer. "What're you looking for?" She didn't seem to hear me.

After a pretty long time she pulled away from the bush. "Farts," she growled.

Wow, I thought, *Marceline McAllister says Farts.* "What's the matter?" I said.

She flicked a pebble with her bare big toe. "They're gone."

"What's gone?"

She didn't answer. She just took off, pumping up the hill. I didn't know what to do. I had the weirdest feeling somewhere around my stomach, like there was a ball of string in there and it was tied to her and as she rode away she was unraveling it.

At the top of the hill she stopped and looked back. She called something, but I couldn't make it out. So I rode all the way up to her. "What?" I said.

"Blackberries," she said, and went zooming down the hill.

I followed.

Pretty soon we were rolling along together. Not side-by-side though — the road was too skinny for that. At first I felt a little funny riding behind a girl like some little puppy dog, but I soon got over that.

Interesting thing about McAllister: take the trombone out of her mouth and put her on a bicycle, and she jabbers away like a thousand parrots. Well, to be honest, I wasn't exactly Silent Sam myself. We pedaled and talked, pedaled and talked. Fences, silos, cows, trees. Mile after mile. When she was doing the talking, I wasn't always listening too well. I couldn't keep my eyes off her bike seat and how perfectly those red shorts of hers fit onto it. Looked something like a big red valentine.

We were chugging up a hill when all of a sudden she points and hollers: "Raccoon!"

I looked just in time to see the striped tail disappear into the bushes. "Neat," I said. "I like raccoons."

"Really?" she said. She seemed shocked.

"Yeah. I like them a lot, as a matter of fact."

"You mean you don't go chasing them and throwing stones at them like all the other idiot boys?"

My brain echoed with the sound of the bottle I threw rattling in the drainpipe, the sound of the soft thud. We were still riding, but her face was turned full around, staring at me, waiting for an answer. I couldn't speak. All the wetness in my throat went to my eyes.

"Yeah, right," she finally sneered, and snapped her head around and pulled away.

I went after her. "Marcy. Marceline. What's the matter? Wha'd I do?"

She glared around again. "*You* tell *me*."

Was I going crazy? There I was, practically trembling in front of this girl, like she was my mother or something, like if I said the wrong thing I'd get spanked. And the craziest thing was, I couldn't lie to her. I wanted to, but I couldn't. "Okay." I shrugged. "So I threw a bottle at one once. So? Is that a crime?"

She skidded to a stop, almost making me crash into her. I was getting the same look from her that I had gotten in the vice-principal's office: burnt toast. "What is it with you boys, anyway? Whenever you see a bird or an animal, anything *alive*, you have to try to kill it. Does it make you feel like a big man, huh? Is that it? Huh?"

I tried to explain, but before three words were out of my mouth she was off again. "Hell with ya," I muttered.

I would have turned back right then, but I hadn't passed any McDonald's, and I figured there *had* to be one up ahead. So I pedaled on — slow — to give her plenty of time to get miles away.

That's why I was surprised only a few minutes later to see her bike parked up against a fence. She was picking something from a tree. I pretended not to notice and cruised on by, but she called, "Peach?"

I U-turned and coasted over. "Nah. I'm waiting for a McDonald's." I reached for my canteen. "Water?"

"Okay," she said. She took about a year wiping the mouth of the canteen with her shirttail — you might have thought I had leprosy — then she took the longest swig I ever saw. In fact, she drank it all. While I gaped in shock, she just grinned and took off, with the canteen. When I finally caught up to her a mile down the road, she was filling the canteen with water running out of a pipe.

"From the water cooler of the earth," she said.

"It's not polluted?"

She just laughed and leaned over and drank right from the pipe. I tried it too. It was the best water I ever had.

We saddled up and moved on. I felt more comfortable when we were riding. On a bicycle she wasn't taller than me.

"I never went past the water pipe before," she said, "but I think you better get a peach next orchard we come to."

"Why?"

"I don't think there's a McDonald's out here."

"Sure there is," I told her. "There's McDonald's everywhere. Wait and see."

"You wait," she said. "I'd rather have a peach anyway."

Shock again. "You don't like McDonald's?"

She snorted. "I hate McDonald's."

I came right out and said it: "Man, you *are* weird."

She just chuckled, so I figured I'd get into a couple other areas I had been wondering about for a long time. "Can I ask you something?" I said.

"Sure."

"Why do you want to be called Marceline?"

"It's my name. What do you want me to be called? Oswalda?"

So much for names. "Whatever made you play the trombone, anyway?"

"Nobody *made* me."

"I mean . . . you know . . ."

"My father plays it."

I wondered if he was a natural or a step. "Don't you feel a little funny playing that thing?" She was silent. Better change the subject. "I hate August," I said.

"I love it," she said.

"You do? Why?"

"Why do you hate it?"

"There's never anybody around."

"So? You afraid to be alone?"

"Course not. Who's talking about being afraid? Anyway, naturally, there's a *couple* people around, but not enough to get a game up. So why are you so crazy about August?"

She stuck out a bare foot and lopped the fuzz off a weed. "Oh, I don't know."

But I figured I knew. Marceline McAllister wasn't popular. Figure it: (1) she insisted on being called Marceline instead of Marcy; (2) she played the trombone; (3) she was tall; (4) she hated McDonald's. Put it this way: she wasn't exactly the Debbie Breen type. So how many friends *could* she have? She *liked* being by herself. And August is a great month for by-yourselfers.

I asked her, "Ever think of cheerleading?"

She slowed down for me to come alongside. The look I got was part burnt toast, part confusion. "Jason," (first time she ever said my name) "what *is* it with you anyway? What did you mean back there about the trombone? Why am I supposed to feel funny playing it?"

"I don't know," I fumbled. How do you explain it?

"You think it's funny to play the trombone, Jason?"

"Nah, it's great." Before I could shut my mouth, a little snicker snuck out.

She snickered back. "Well, do *you* feel funny?"

"Huh? About what?"

"Killing raccoons?"

I glared right at her and yelled. "I don't kill no raccoons!"

"Being short?"

An icicle stabbed me. I didn't know it was that obvious. Did she know I didn't have pubic hair too?

"Being made a fool of?" she sneered.

"Yeah? By who?"

She rolled her eyes up and sighed. "Oh, by a certain Miss Breen."

"I didn't see anybody asking *you* to dance, skinny."

"Oh, yes, Jason dear, I'd love to see your space station. I'll come tomorrow. Or maybe the day after tomorrow. If I don't have a toothache. I get a lot of toothaches, you know."

"How many boys are after *you*, Mar-*cee*?"

"Jason dear, why did you run away on Halloween? That tiny little Luke Skywalker *was* you, wasn't it?"

"Ever see the wall in the girls locker room, Mar-*cee*?"

"So that's where you hang out."

"It says Marceline McAllister sucks trombones."

"Boo-hoo."

"You think you're the greatest thing in the world."

"Thank you."

"Well, you're not! You're an asshole and everybody knows it!"

"That so?"

"Yeah, that's so! Nobody likes you!"

"My mother does.'

"Up yours, Mar-*ceel*"

"Twerp."

"Everybody knows what you do with that trombone every night! Mar-*ceel*"

"Runt."

"The fudge I gave you that time had ants in it!"

"I hope they were pissants like you."

"Mar-*ceel* Mar-*ceel* Mar-*ceel* Mar-*ceel* Mar-*ceel* Mar-*ceel*"

"Raccoon killer."

"I don't kill raccoons!"

"Short immature runt raccoon killer."

She was laughing.

"Knock it off!" I screamed. "I ain't no raccoon killer! I love raccoons! I felt rotten ever since I threw the bottle at that one! I gave my Valentine's candy to Esther Kufel! I teach little kids stuff! I can't sleep right ever since Peter Kim's little brother got killed! I'm a good kid! You hear? My stepfather says so! I'M A GOOD KID!!"

She was wheeling away, hunching over and pumping like a demon. I got into my racing form and took off after her, screaming bloody murder all the while. She zipped out of sight around a sharp curve and all of a sudden I heard a scream, a crash, and a moo, and I screeched to a halt in front of the craziest scene I ever saw: she had crashed into a cow.

The front of her bike was caved in, Marceline was sprawled and whimpering on the ground, and the cow was just standing there like a dope. There was a tire mark on its side.

Marceline reached for her floppy red hat — *red* hat! — I grabbed her and dragged her away. "Look out!" I warned. "Maybe it's a bull!"

She got to her feet, sneering. "That's no bull, dumbo." She pointed downward. "Look."

These pink and white udders were hanging down all over. They were humongous. I felt myself blushing. "So?" I said. "Maybe bulls have them too."

She sighed at the sky. "Oh God."

Well, bull or cow, somehow we managed to get the animal back through the break in the fence and into the field. That's when I noticed her arm: it was bleeding. I froze. Not because it was a bad cut, but because of the fence that cut her — it was barbed wire, and it was rusty. *Lockjaw!*

I tried to act casual. "Hey, uh, looks like you got a little nick there."

She looked. By the way she said "Uh-oh" I could tell she knew about lockjaw too. "Got a hankie?" she asked me.

I did, but it was full of boogies. Anyway, that wasn't the treatment. "You gotta suck it," I told her.

She made a face. Then she held out her arm, right under my nose. The cut was on the inside of her arm. The skin was real white there. *Don't think*, I told myself, *just do it*. Next thing I know I'm sucking and spitting like crazy. I'm trying to suck as hard as I can, since I figure the poison's got a head start, but the problem is, the harder I suck the more scared I get that I'm going to suck the poison right down my own throat. So I spitted about twenty times for each suck.

Finally she goes, "Owww!" and snatches her arm away. "That's e-*nuff*."

"Gotta — get — it all — out," I gasped.

"You were *biting*."

"I was not biting. I was sucking." My face was getting warm. (I swear, I *wasn't* biting.)

"Well, isn't that enough?"

We both looked down at her arm — and my face switched to hot. There it was, all around the cut, purple and red: a hickey. Just like the ones you see on The Lovers' necks all the time.

I acted like I didn't notice. "Yeah," I said, "that's enough."

Her bike was totaled. We left it there and started walking. It was pretty grim. Nobody said much. Every once in a while I'd try something like, "Too bad about your bike," or "The cow didn't even have a dent." The most she would do was grunt. Other than that the only sound was the click-click of my bike wheels.

Fields that we zipped by before took forever to pass now. We walked and walked and walked and I couldn't believe we still didn't come to the water pipe. The sun fell behind the treetops. I couldn't believe we had gone so far without seeing a McDonald's. We stopped to pick some peaches. Pretty soon the sun looked like a giant peach perched on top of the corn.

Now I was really getting nervous. A plum-colored mist was settling into the valleys. I pictured my mother — or would it be Ham? — calling the police. Sirens. Walkie-talkie voices. Radio description . . . *last seen on yellow ten-speed . . . thirteen years old . . . brown hair . . . none in pubic area or underarms . . . short. . . .* Mary bawling, "*He was the best brother anybody ever had!*"

The moon was a white toenail clipping in the sky. The cars had their headlights on. I knew what I had to do. "Marcy — Marceline," I said, "our parents — they're gonna be all bent."

She shrugged. "So?"

"So, they'll think we're missing persons. They'll call the cops."

"So?"

"So, we gotta hurry. We gotta ride." I stopped and climbed onto my bike. I patted the bar in front of me. "Get on."

She got on. I could hardly believe it. I guess cracking up her bike and cutting herself took the fight out of her.

The downhills were great, but the uphills — they were the killers. I threw my bike into first, and still I had to pump hard. I tried to keep the sound of my breath down. I would stop breathing for twenty or thirty seconds, but the breaths would bunch up and burst out all at once and I'd go, "Paaahh!"

Sometimes going downhill her hair would come streaming back into my face. I didn't brush it away.

Once I said to her, "What's a trombone weigh?" She said that was a dumb question and how should she know — but that was good enough for me. She didn't know I was just checking to make sure her jaw wasn't starting to lock up.

At last we came to the water pipe. "Let's have a snort," she said. Gratefully, I pulled over. She got off and took a drink. I did too, and when I turned around she was on my bike, on the seat.

"Oh no," I told her. "No way. *I'm* driving."

"Jason, get on."

"Nope."

"Jason, you drove half the way, now I'll do the rest. It's only fair."

"Nope."

"Jason, you were wobbling all over the place. Now get on."

"I was not wobbling."

"Jason, stop being a macho piglet! *Get on!*" She reached out and grabbed my ear and pulled and twisted and wouldn't let go till I was seated on the crossbar.

"By the way," she said, "thanks."

"Thanks?" I screeched, untwisting my poor ear. "For what?"

"For your lip surgery on my arm," she grinned, and we took off.

The stars had all joined the moon and it was really dark out now. At first all I could think about was what if one of the guys saw me being ridden along on my own bike — by a girl. But then I started to think about other stuff, mostly her. She was as hard to figure out as the world. She was a girl, but she could ride a bike like a boy. She loved animals, but she hated McDonald's. She busted her gut running the mile, but she cried when she crashed into cows. She was tall, but in some ways she was little too. There was a whole mishmash of thoughts and feelings about her churning inside me, and I wasn't sure about any of them. One thing I *was* sure of, though: no way could they be written down on a locker room wall.

I was thinking about these things when she pulled off the road. "Excuse me," she said, getting off, "I have to pee." Just like that. Off she went into the bushes, while my face did a great imitation of a red giant star.

When she came back she took a swig of water. This time she didn't bother to wipe off the mouth of the canteen before she drank.

"Jason?" she said once we were rolling again.

"Yeah?"

"The raccoon's not dead."

"What about the bottle?" I said. "I heard it hit."

"The raccoon is okay."

I don't know — just the way her voice sounded, just because it was *her* saying it — it sounded true. It *felt* true. "You sure?" I said.

"I'm sure."

I kind of settled back then, relaxed. I was really enjoying the ride. The hills were flattening out and we were mostly cruising. In the distance I could see the faint glow of the town. I wished it was still five hundred miles away.

I heard a sound behind me, a soft, beautiful sound. She was humming.

I tilted my head back so that all I could see was the sky. The universe. I remembered my dream, of how *Pioneer* came to my bedroom window and waited for me to put something on board. Suddenly I knew what I would do. The gold figures of the man and woman from Earth — I would etch two names in the gold beneath them:

JASON   MARCELINE

And we would go sailing out to the stars.